This
Day
in
History

The

John

Simmons

Short

Fiction

Award

University of

Iowa Press

Iowa City

*Anthony
Varallo*

---

*This Day
in History*

University of Iowa Press, Iowa City 52242

http://www.uiowa.edu/uiowapress

The publication of this book was generously supported by the National Endowment for the Arts.

The University of Iowa Press is a member of Green Press Initiative and is committed to preserving natural resources. Printed on acid-free paper

Library of Congress Cataloging-in-Publication Data

Varallo, Anthony, 1970 – .

This day in history / Anthony Varallo.

p.   cm. — (John Simmons short fiction award)

ISBN 0-87745-951-7 (pbk.)

1. Boys—Fiction.   2. United States—Social life and customs—Fiction. I. Title.   II. Series.

PS3622.A725T48 2005

813'.6—dc22   2005045703

05 06 07 08 09 P 5 4 3 2 1

For Malinda and Gus,

and for my family

Contents

ACKNOWLEDGMENTS

I would like to thank the editors of the magazines in which these stories first appeared: "The Eyes of Dr. T. J. Eckleburg" in the *Bellingham Review*; "The Pines" in the *Journal*; "A Tiny Raft" in *Boulevard*; "Pool Season" in *Epoch*; "Sunday Wash" in *Crazyhorse*; "The Miles between Harriet Tubman and Harry Truman" in the *Greensboro Review*; "The Houses Left Behind" in *Black Warrior Review*; "A Dictionary of Saints" in *Crazyhorse*; "The Knot" in *Mississippi Review*; "Be True to Your School" in the *Sun*; "Sometimes I'm Becky Macomber" in *Sundog: The Southeast Review*; and "This Day in History" in *River City*. "The Pines" was selected by Lee K. Abbot as the winner in the *Journal*'s First Annual Short Story Award, and "Sunday Wash" was selected by Charles Baxter as the winner of the 2002 *Crazyhorse* Fiction Prize.

I would also like to thank the many wonderful creative writing teachers I've had over the years, especially Bernard Kaplan, Frank Conroy, Jim McPherson, Marilynne Robinson, Marly Swick, Trudy Lewis, and Speer Morgan. A special thanks to the University of Iowa Writers' Workshop and the University of Missouri-Columbia for their time and encouragement, to the National Endowment for the Arts for their support, and to the University of Iowa Press for all their work in bringing this book together.

I could not have written these stories without the help of my friends, readers, and fellow writers, nor without the support of my wife, Malinda McCollum, who is all three and more. Lastly, I'd like to thank our son, Gus, who helps us turn the pages.

This
Day
in
History

The
Eyes of
Dr. T. J. Eckleburg

Ben Palazzo never finished *The Great Gatsby*. His brother died two weeks before we were to graduate from eighth grade, and I never saw him again. His brother Mark, away at college, had hung himself from a chin-up bar. It was in the newspaper. It was on the school announcements, right before intramural soccer scores and cap-and-gown reminders. We had a moment of silence during the graduation ceremony, after Brother Richard delivered a speech about our future, which was, he said, like a hot air balloon rising into a wide sky.

Ben lived in the development across from mine. We rode the bus together, our knees to the seat in front of us, playing a video football game where a red hyphen ran hopelessly against four defensive hyphens, their moves accompanied by a faint ticking noise. *Tick-tick*. Sometimes I'd spend the weekend at Ben's house and sometimes he'd spend the weekend at mine, but it was always more fun at Ben's since his mother didn't mind if we stayed up all night eating potato chips and watching television. They had the best snack foods. Most weekends we sat in front of Ben's VCR, where Ben had rigged a microphone to the input jack, recording our voices over the Million Dollar Movie.

"Why is my tie so big?" Ben had Bogey say, in *Casablanca*.

"Stop talking about your tie," my Ingrid Bergman warned. "Look at my *hat*!"

A girl lived across the street from Ben. Her name was Carolyn. Carolyn was three years older than us, a high school girl, yet mysteriously friends with Ben. Once we hung out in her driveway while she affixed bumper stickers to her dashboard. One read "My Karma Ran Over Your Dogma." She told me I looked like someone who collected coins. She had the nicest teeth.

———————

Daisy is the girl in *The Great Gatsby*. The woman. She's frivolous, silly, but Gatsby loves her anyway. He's crazy about her. He throws huge parties hoping she'll come over. He buys her flowers. That's the whole point of the book: Gatsby could have anything in the world but the one thing he truly wanted, Daisy.

"Oh, Daisy!" he said.

"Oh, Jay!" Daisy said. They talked this way. Nick couldn't understand why Gatsby would want Daisy. He felt sorry for him. I liked it that Nick felt sorry for Gatsby. If I were Nick, I'd be the exact same way.

Poor Gatsby! Nick says.

Poor Gatsby! I'd say.

The first time we went to Carolyn's, we brought her a stuffed animal monkey. We'd been abusing the monkey for the purpose of a video, shot by me, narrated by Ben. "No one knows the depths of the commode," Ben said, Vincent Price–like, then lowered the monkey into the toilet and closed the lid upon its grinning head. "Bru-hah-hah-ha-ha!" We put the monkey in Ben's deep freeze; the monkey emerged unfazed, although the squeaker inside his tongue refused to sound. We put the monkey on a dart-board. We tied his arms to a file cabinet and dropped the cabinet from a fairly significant height. We dunked him in turpentine.

"We're torturing this monkey," Ben said.

Carolyn stood in the doorway. She looked at us like we were explaining how to fold towels. "That's hardly nice," she said. "Hardly nice at all." Her indifference impressed me until I remembered I still held the video camera. She knew how to act.

"Say something to the camera," Ben said.

"I hide the wire that watches the one you want," she said.

"Carolyn's weird," Ben said. He introduced us.

I felt dumb about the video camera and the monkey. "I feel dumb," I said.

"Do you?" Carolyn said.

"About the camera," I said.

"He feels dumb about the video camera," Ben said.

"Stop talking about the video camera," Carolyn said.

There's a feeling I get whenever I enter an unfamiliar house, as if a secret inventory has been handed to me, and I am made to understand that the sofa cushions are stained underneath, the coffee table nursing one gimp leg, the books along the bookcase stolen from a summer rental, and the dining room table used only for Christmas and taxes. Then the feeling passes and the room becomes only a room again, where, perhaps, *World News Tonight* is on television. This inventory lingered longer when I entered Carolyn's house, and I somehow felt I understood her life all at once. She was unhappy. Her parents were unhappy. Her brothers and sisters, all older, married, or away at college, were also unhappy. They rarely visited, except at Thanksgiving or Christmas, but these were moody occasions, with everyone staring drearily into the old Sylvania television, which still wasn't hooked up to cable, and still cropped Peter Jennings's head at the top, as it had done when they were children. The meal was under- and/or over-cooked and left an aftertaste of frozen butter. A freshly poured glass of Pepsi, arriving from the kitchen, dissipated into nearly nothing, and seemed a deliberate rebuke.

"I like your mirror," I said. An enormous, gilt-framed mirror hung above the credenza, in which I could now see the three of us.

"You do?" Carolyn said. "That's funny. My dad stole that mirror from a hotel. We were on vacation. I was in first grade. He said, 'Sugarpie, how'd you'd like to take that mirror home?' I said I didn't care. He said, 'You'll like this mirror once you get used to it. You'll think it's the best thing since Pop Tarts.'" Carolyn glanced at herself in the mirror. "I had to keep one hand on it as we drove away, to keep it from falling off the roof. My mother refused to ride with us. A year later, she died."

"Your mother isn't dead," Ben said.

"Up to a certain point," Carolyn said.

We sat in Carolyn's kitchen, watching TV. I kept trying to figure out why we'd gone there in the first place. Carolyn didn't seem to like Ben very much. She twirled a napkin into rope while he recounted the plots of movies he'd seen. Once, she stood up and left the room for twenty minutes while Ben and I stared into the TV and debated whether she was coming back or not. "She'll be back eventually," Ben said, which was true, since we were in her house, but I didn't say anything. I looked at Ben. He sat with his hands atop the kitchen table, sucking in his cheeks. He did that sometimes. I had to admit, he looked sort of good doing it. Ben was nice looking, people said.

Ben had known Carolyn for years. Their families shared a beach house where, the summer before, Ben and Carolyn had stolen a shopping cart and pushed it into the ocean, an act of such easy vandalism that Ben returned to it again and again, searching for its mislaid complexity. "We had to lift it over a sand lot and push it along a dirt road," he'd explained, breathlessly, the night we got back from Carolyn's. We were sleeping in his living room, which his mother had fitted out with two glass cases of antique dolls; we made a game of putting our faces to the glass, whispering, "Tonight, I keeeel you both, oh yes"; and for this reason a smiling, moonish face hung palely in my mind as Ben rhapsodized about hiding the cart behind a sand dune and feeling Carolyn's breath along his shoulder. "She told me to quit laughing, but I couldn't. It was just too funny, you know?" I said I knew. "She was all like 'Shutup!' but I was like 'I can't!'" I pictured Carolyn's face the moment she'd returned to the kitchen and found us scooping ice from the freezer. "There's too much copper in the ice water," she said. "Makes everything taste like old pennies."

"Or new pennies," I'd said. I was glad I'd said that.

"It was so dark when we pushed it off the pier I almost went with it," Ben said. "That's the thing I remember most, how dark it was."

How dark it was, I thought. Ben's story reminded me of why I liked him in the first place: he thought in stories. It was also the thing I liked least about him. The feeling of someone else using your toothbrush.

That night Ben whispered, "I've messed around with her."

"You lie," I said.

"No lie."

"When?"

"At the beach. At her house."

"Lie and lie."

"No. True and true."

Before we left Carolyn's house, she had shown us her father's high school yearbook. "He hates when I do this," she said, then flipped to a photograph of the boys' track team. Boys with crew-cut hair, shoulder to shoulder in the long shadow of the football stands. "This is him," she said, "and *this* is none other than Mr. Elvis Aaron Presley."

I looked. A boy with dark hair, glasses.

"Yeah, right," Ben said. "*That's* Elvis."

"It is, indeed."

"On the track team," Ben laughed.

"Elected co-captain."

"But," I said, already wishing I hadn't, "it says 'E. Preston' underneath. And this yearbook is from the 60s. I think Elvis was already famous by then."

"Are you saying you don't believe me?" Carolyn asked.

"No, but."

"He means yes," Ben said.

Carolyn clapped the yearbook closed. "You, sir, are afraid of possibility," she said. "The both of you."

My house faced a cul-de-sac, whose lone basketball hoop had shed its net, and whose backboard shakily supported a wasp's nest, holed like a harmonica. I liked to shoot baskets there after school, using a crack in the pavement as a foul line. I'd stand at the line and make my shot, keeping stats. I liked stats. I liked the idea of reporting them to Mr. Dawes, our gym teacher, who would, I'd imagine, raise his eyebrow at 6 for 10, 13 for 20. I imagined him writing these numbers into a yellow legal pad, then tapping a pen across its top. "That's nice work, son," he'd say. Evenings, I did my homework at the kitchen table, facing two sliding glass doors whose reflection showed me studiously chewing a Ticonderoga or tidying the margins of a torn notepage. At night I slept with windows open and thought of Carolyn. What did she see in Ben?

I'd done something the night we visited her, something I hadn't told Ben. It was when I asked to use the bathroom. I closed the door and washed my hands, twice. I put my hands through my hair and practiced looking bored but wise, jaded but withholding awe. It was a tiny bathroom, showerless and festively grim, with a glass potpourri jar perched atop the toilet tank, where a significant crack had been mended with packing tape. The potpourri smelled like damp stones. I didn't want to stay, but I didn't want to leave, either. I imagined Carolyn and me hanging out, laughing about the bathroom—*can you believe this bathroom?*—but I knew this was a dumb thing to imagine, so I toweled my hands, then dropped a St. Francis of Assisi medallion, a trinket I'd been keeping in my wallet, into the potpourri jar. I don't know why I did that. When I returned to the kitchen, Ben was standing in front of the refrigerator, posing like a bodybuilder. "I thought you were Carolyn," he said.

The first time I met Ben was in after-school detention. He'd been jugged for faking his mom's signature, and I was serving for clapping erasers in the hallway. I liked the way the dust caught in the light. I was just getting into it when Brother Joseph appeared, dangling his coffee cup from his pale fingers. "Well, I wish I hadn't seen that," he said.

"Me, too," I said. I liked Brother Joseph. He was a teller of knock-knock jokes and a lousy disciplinarian. He kept a wooden chess set inside his desk and sometimes tossed the pieces to us when we weren't paying enough attention.

"Do you think you're becoming the kind of person who gets into trouble?"

"No, Brother."

"I'll tell you a story," he said. "When I was seventeen my aunt Rita begged me not to join the seminary. I mean *begged*. She even threw a party and invited all the prettiest girls from the neighborhood, hoping I'd change my mind. I remember her crying as I played pinochle with Mary Beth McIntyre. Mary Beth was very pretty, of course, and I was very much attracted to her, of course, and wanted to please my aunt, but. You see what I'm getting at."

"Yes, Brother."

"My aunt was a remarkable woman, a true mother to me. Uncle Paul, like a father. He was a quiet man. Silent, almost. Sometimes I'd find him curled up on the sofa with his eyes closed, just praying and praying. That made an impression."

"Yes, Brother."

"After he died we always remembered him at Thanksgiving. You see, Uncle Paul had a theory that it was best to butter your corn by using a fork instead of a knife, so that the fork held the butter, allowing it to melt through. There isn't a Thanksgiving that goes by that someone doesn't say, 'Remember the way Paul used to butter his corn? With a *fork*.' But you see what I'm getting at." Brother Joseph put a hand on my shoulder. "Isn't it amazing," he said, "what we might be remembered for?"

During detention I sat at a long, damply wiped table and tried to read *Gatsby* for a while, but it was no use. I kept getting stuck on the scene where Tom takes Nick to meet his girlfriend. They go into town. Someone sells them a puppy. Everyone has too much to drink. Tom's girlfriend says "Daisy, Daisy, Daisy" and Tom punches her. It didn't make sense to me somehow, and I kept flipping back to the cover, looking for clues. I liked that, when you saw clues. Like the way a movie poster looks to you before going in: you see a pelican sitting at the star's feet and think, *Oh, a pelican*, only to learn that the pelican steals the show by hiding a rare diamond in its beak, so that leaving the theater, you see the pelican again and think, *There he is!* I wanted something like that to happen with the *Gatsby* cover.

"Do you know what this is?" Ben whispered.

"No," I said. Ben was sitting across from me, reading a coffee table book whose cover showed the Hindenburg raining fire on a New Jersey field. *Disaster!* the book was called.

"It's my little sunshine book," Ben said, then laughed without making any noise.

So I liked him well enough. If friendship is more decision than feeling, we were friends. I sat with him at lunch and laughed at things that weren't funny. I adopted his habit of sticking nickels between the trim of my Docksiders. Sometimes I imagined myself as him, so that the ordinariness of setting a fork beside a plate or kneeling at the communion rail took on the burnish of a spy mission. I wore the collar of my windbreaker up. I parted my hair in the middle.

But mostly I thought of Carolyn. I tried to think of her and Ben kissing, walking along a moonlit beach, Ben making jokes, writing their initials in the sand with a broken shell. There was a feeling there, inside the idea of them kissing, but I couldn't figure it out. Jealousy, sure, because Carolyn was pretty and Ben was Ben and because I had never kissed a girl, but something else, too. Whenever I thought of them, I thought of Carolyn's house. I thought of its drab carpet and heavy curtains, its golden mirror crookedly hanging above the dining room credenza. You could see Carolyn's house from Ben's bathroom window, which was always slightly open, and which I sometimes opened wider, peering into Carolyn's yard. A tree blocked my view of Carolyn's bedroom, where I'd always hoped to see her undressing. Twin floodlights cast bright light upon the driveway. A red bike leaned against the front porch, the porch sheltering a wood pile, whose pieces has been stacked into rows, like wine bottles. A high-top sneaker hung from a low branch, tossed there, I guessed, by one of Carolyn's friends. These objects, brilliant in the floodlights, felt unnaturally precious to me, as if they were somehow mine. As if I'd left them behind.

One weekend Ben and I walked around his neighborhood, talking into a toy microphone. It was the end of April. Lawns were just beginning to be lawns again. Ben spoke into the microphone in a deep voice. "People of Earth," he said, "this is the Lord your God with a special message just for you: Hankity-spankity-wankity!"

Passing a house where a gray cat slept atop a black trampoline: "Attention, Citizens of Westminster Green. Everyone leave the neighborhood immediately. We're having it dry cleaned!"

We stopped at the neighborhood park, where there was a dome-shaped jungle gym we'd once nearly flipped before two moms showed up, pushing babies in bright strollers. I climbed to the top and watched Ben slip his legs through a triangular opening cut into the air like a can's spout. "My Fellow Americans," Ben said, hanging from his knees, "I have a confession to make. I'm made entirely of sausage!" I could see the half-moons of Ben's nostrils, whose middles pinched together when he laughed. His legs, hooked around the triangle's hypotenuse, brought his feet close to mine. His shoelaces were untied. I grabbed Ben's foot.

"Hey!"

I raised his leg. He looked up at me.

"Don't."

"Try holding on," I said.

"Can't," Ben said.

"Figure something out."

"Don't!"

But I did. Except that Ben's hand shot out from his coat sleeve and gripped a lower bar. "Aha," he said. He freed his other leg, swung it to the ground, and landed with both hands gripping lower bars, like someone pushing a car from a snowdrift. The microphone cracked open, dislodging its slender batteries. "Asshole."

I looked down at Ben. He brushed dirt from his knees and straightened his shirt. You had to have times like these, I thought, feeling a sudden, terrific hope. Had to test the limb to prove the solidity of the tree.

When we returned to Ben's house, his brother's car was in the driveway. "Oh, great," Ben said. "Just great." I had never met Mark before, but knew enough not to bring up his name around Ben. One time I'd asked him what Mark was studying in college and Ben made a drinking motion with his fist. "Oh, a little of this," he said, then pretended to touch himself, "and that." We found Mark on the family room sofa, a blanket drawn to his head, which was capped with a red-and-white winter hat, an asterisk of cut yarn drooping from its peak. He turned away when we entered the room.

"Hey, Mark," Ben said.

"Hey," Mark said.

"Nice hat."

"*Danke.*"

"Do mom and dad know you're here?"

"No more than you know you're here," Mark said. He turned to face us, but only lowered the blanket to his nose. "Did you hear that? That's the way you'll talk in college. Irony." He cleared his throat. "You'll be the funniest person you've ever known."

"Jim's funny," Ben said, but Mark didn't say anything. I elbowed Ben. "Come on."

"You'll have so many funny friends," Mark said. "And they'll all be geniuses, *just like you.*"

I heard a clock, then noticed one of those clocks that spin their insides like a pinwheel sitting atop the mantle.

"Did you go upstairs yet?" Ben said. "Mom moved all of her sewing stuff into your old room."

Mark laughed. "To sew a brand-new son."

"She said she wants you to go through the boxes in the closet. I told her you'd be mad if she threw anything away."

"A regular brother's keeper."

"You should go up there and see. She almost threw away your snare drum."

"Then realized it was something else to hold against me."

It wasn't until we'd gotten upstairs, where Ben made a pretense of flipping through his record collection, that I realized he'd cried a little. "This is like the best album ever," Ben said, then dropped the Stones' *Beggar's Banquet* onto the turntable we'd once rigged as a torture wheel for his Smurfs. Ben shook hairbrush maracas to "Sympathy for the Devil" and crooned along with Mick, which embarrassed me. I took a squirrel puppet from Ben's bookshelf and had the squirrel say "nut" over every fifth word or so, which was enough to break him up. Outside, it was just getting dark. I thought of Carolyn's house with its porch light not yet on. It always made me depressed to see her house without the porch light on.

Later, Ben said, "You know what I think about sometimes? It's totally stupid, but I think about what it would be like if I had to live in my bedroom for a while. Like if the door locked and the windows wouldn't open. If I had to be in here for a week."

"Like if there was a giant snowstorm," I offered.

"Right. All trapped inside."

"It'd be fun until you had to use the bathroom."

"There'd be bathroom breaks," Ben said.

"What about food?"

"Someone would bring it in," Ben said, "on a tray."

Nick and Gatsby aren't really friends. Nick doesn't even recognize Gatsby when he first meets him. He has no idea. Then Gatsby says, "I'm Gatsby," and Nick feels dumb. The next day they go for a ride on Gatsby's boat. Nick doesn't know what to think of him. "Old sport," Gatsby calls him. Nick likes that. Old sport.

The last night I ever saw Carolyn was the night Ben stole wine from his parents' refrigerator. The wine came inside a little white box whose outside bore a photograph of glistening red grapes, and from whose front a gray spout protruded like a pig's snout. It was the kind of wine we always had in our house, too: pink Chablis, for special occasions like Easter and first communions, when relatives stood around the kitchen table, dragging Wheat Thins through spinach dip and nearly hitting their heads on the kitchen light, suspended by a clunky chain, which we always forgot to hitch up to the ceiling, as an uncle invariably would, saying, "Now, we're cooking." Ben and I took turns drinking the wine. "Ah," Ben said, smacking his lips. "I do believe, I say, I do believe I am inebriated."

"Moving pianos," I said, reviving one of our routines. "Dat is the wuhrst."

"Moooving pianos," Ben said.

"The ab-so-lute wuhrst," I said, trying to sound drunk. One of the things I was most afraid of was that I would never truly get drunk. I sometimes imagined explaining this to a doctor who would, I believed, nod his head while writing something on a clipboard.

"You should see your mouth when you talk like that," Ben said. "It gets all weird."

We walked around Ben's neighborhood, where Ben finished the wine, then threw the box into a pond, where it refused to sink. "Find a rock," Ben said. I found three, and handed him one. "Perfect." He lobbed the rock toward the box, but missed. "You try," he said. I tried to skip mine into the box, but it sailed over the top. "If I hit the box with this rock," Ben said, "that means I'll live to be one hundred." He missed, but picked up another rock and missed again. The next rock hit the box squarely, a direct hit. "Well, goddamn," Ben said.

We arrived at Carolyn's house. Carolyn was wearing green slippers and a blue nightgown with glossy sunflowers shimmering across its front. "I skipped school today," she said.

"Are you sick?" I said.

"In theory," Carolyn said. "If not in fact."

"What did you do all day?" Ben asked.

"First I sat in my room, doing nothing, then I went downstairs and did nothing there. I kind of got into it. Not doing anything. I tried to go outside, but then I felt guilty about it, like I should at least act like I was sick. So I sat in front of the TV and did crossword puzzles instead." Carolyn sighed. "Sometimes I feel like I'm the world's youngest senior citizen."

"I know what you mean," Ben said.

"I can't wait to retire," Carolyn said.

"Yeah," I said. "I want to get a boat."

We went upstairs and hung out in Carolyn's bedroom, thrilling to me. It was the first time I had ever been in a girl's bedroom. There was a twin bed with folded clothes heaped on top, a nightstand with T-shirts spilling from its drawers, a Who poster tacked to a bulletin board, a desk and a chair, and a black beanbag that Ben dropped into like a shagged fly ball. A white dresser grew an oblong mirror from its middle, its corners jammed with postcards and photographs: "Greetings from Rehoboth!"; Carolyn and two other girls dressed as cheerleaders, middle fingers raised; Jack Nicholson's grinning head filling the gash of an axed door; the Dalai Lama; a child's drawing of a girl with long hair.

"Hey, what's with the giraffe?" Ben asked.

Beside the bed stood a giraffe, four feet tall, composed entirely of popsicle sticks.

"Don't ask me about the giraffe," Carolyn said.

"Did you make it?" Ben asked.

"I don't want to talk about the giraffe."

I sat at Carolyn's desk and listened to Ben and Carolyn talk about music. Ben seemed to know things about hidden messages, backward tracks, and album covers that, held to a mirror, revealed secret telephone numbers. "The devil's number," Ben said.

"Always busy, I bet," Carolyn said.

There was a feeling of being in Carolyn's bedroom, new to me, of peering behind a screen and glimpsing someone undressing. A sense of skin, nakedness, and sweat. This had been the room I'd hoped to see, on those evenings when I looked through the bathroom window, the distance between houses narrowed, in my mind, by the sheer power of my desire. How many times had I thought of this very room, of being in it, alone with Carolyn, without having any idea what it was like? How many times had I thought of kissing her, touching her? Everything I had wished for, Carolyn's room now informed me, was insubstantial and vague. I'd hoped for—what? her socks asked, balled into like colors and spilling from her drawer. I knew so little, her curtains suggested, drawn back by white ropes, tied into bows. Close your eyes, a purple bra commanded, hanging from a doorknob. I felt my face grow warm.

"Do you think everyone is your friend?" Carolyn asked me later, while Ben dozed on the beanbag.

"I don't know," I said. "I guess not."

"I always used to think everyone was my friend," Carolyn said. "When I was your age."

I didn't like Carolyn saying it, mostly because it was true. I *did* think everyone was my friend. "I have lots of enemies," I said.

"Like who?"

"Like Ben," I said, and Carolyn laughed.

"You could be, too," I said.

"I'm lots of people's enemy," Carolyn said.

"I was just kidding."

"No," Carolyn said. "It's a long list."

Later, Carolyn opened her window and asked me to retrieve a Frisbee that had gotten stuck on the roof. "I wouldn't ask you if you weren't my dearest enemy," she said. She blew me a kiss.

"You should ask Ben," I said.

"Ask me what?" Ben muttered.

"To be my dearest enemy," Carolyn said, but I was already on the roof. It was nice out there. I couldn't remember the last time I'd been on a roof, the pebbly feel of shingles beneath my feet, the moon a fat ornament hung from an unseen branch. I scooted toward the edge and saw the Frisbee sticking out of the gutter like a refused coin. "It's in the gutter," I said. "I can't reach."

"Try grabbing it with your feet," Carolyn said. I looked back and saw her watching me from the window, where Ben's face hovered just beyond her shoulder. It occurred to me that the two of them were watching me with the idea that I might fall. I slid closer to the Frisbee, touching it with my sneaker. Across the street I could see Ben's house, lit from inside, and the house next to his, bordered by poplars. But I could see beyond them, too, to other houses, other streets, other neighborhoods. "Got it," I said. But I hadn't yet.

A billboard watches over Tom and Daisy, Gatsby and Nick. It is the billboard that presides over the valley of ashes, a monstrous pair of blue eyes behind yellow glasses, the eyes of Dr. T. J. Eckleburg. The billboard that watches the valley where Tom's mistress dies, the death blamed on Gatsby. Everything that happens, happens within its sight. So my rooftop view seemed to me, a vast valley charged with mystery and consequence.

"Here," I said, then tossed the Frisbee to Carolyn.

"Thanks."

"It's amazing out here."

"Look for a hockey stick, a push broom, and a tennis ball, too," Carolyn said. "I threw everything I could at the fucker."

Here is the last thing I remember about that night. We returned late to Ben's house and found Mark sleeping in the family room. We could see the shape of him on the sofa. We could see his feet, his middle, the peak of his hat. But when Ben accidentally stumbled into a magazine rack, the shape did not move. Ben flicked the lights on. The sofa was a pile of pillows and blankets, arranged to look like a body. A trick.

"Ha," Ben said, then lifted the blanket in mock astonishment. "Mark? Are you in here?"

"Are you in here?" I said, lifting a cushion.

Ben opened the coffee table drawers. "How about here? Mark?"

"Mark, is that you?" I said, placing my hands on the television screen. "Are you okay?"

We laughed. We got into it.

"Shout if you can hear us!" Ben said into a cookie tin. "Let us know."

"We need to know, Mark," I said, then rapped on the screen.

"He could be anywhere," Ben said.

"He could be in the stereo," I said.

"He could."

We allowed a moment for the stereo to clear its throat, the television to rub its eyes, and the sofa, stripped of cushions, to gather itself together. I'd never noticed how empty a sofa looked that way. All along, I'd thought there were feathers underneath.

The Pines

A few weeks after the holidays, Derek Trotter wrestled our Christmas tree from the trash and drove it to Campfire Lake, where Tank, the biggest catfish in the state, was once videotaped swallowing a tossed pinecone. I watched Derek from my bedroom window; I had just finished reading my sister's diary—it had a flimsy brass "lock" that opened when you turned a paper clip inside it. The diary had been my father's Christmas gift to her, but so far she'd only written a page.

When Derek knocked, I answered the door. "Are you going to be using this?" he asked. He gestured toward the tree, already bungeed into the trunk. "Anymore?" He wore a blue ski mask with stitched reindeer gamboling around its top.

"No," I said. "I think we're all done with it." I tried not to notice his mask, which was like trying not to notice yourself in a mirror. He was sixteen and known around the neighborhood as something of a bully.

"You should be," he said. "I mean, it's almost Valentine's Day."

"I know," I said.

"I mean, what the hell, right?"

"Right," I said. His eyes were pink-lidded, flecked with crust. I'd heard that Derek Trotter had once blinded his sister with a paintball gun.

"You gonna need that tree on Valentine's Day? Is that the plan? Give it to your girlfriend?" His laugh was like a stomped balloon. "Like, 'Here honey, this's for you.'"

"No," I said.

"Because that's one lame gift," he said. He spat into the geranium pot in which nothing had flowered for months. "You let me know if you see any more trees."

I considered this. "Okay."

"I mean it." His voice drifted into a minor key. "I need them." When Derek pulled away, I could see our tree juddering against the trunk.

It was our first Christmas since our parents split, and we'd forgotten about the tree until February. It had been my father's job to do that kind of thing: liberate the tree from the stand, drag it to the end of the driveway, and lean it against our Rubbermaid trash cans, whose lids quietly refused to seal the summer after he moved away. Now it was up to me to replace blown fuses, flatten spiders that noiselessly toured the tub, and saw the lowest branches of the Christmas tree so that the stand would accept its width. I had chopped one branch, then the next, then another, trying to make the bottom even, but only ended up making the tree look strangely bare underneath, like a bride raising her hem.

My father taught art at a local high school. He had been a painter in New York for a while, but things hadn't worked out, and he'd fallen in love with my mother in the midst of his disappointment and married her too quickly. Or so our mother said. "Sometimes I wonder if we're ever really supposed to leave home," she once told me, when we were watching a movie I was too young to follow. In it, a woman ran across a grassy field while black planes passed overhead. "Whose idea was that anyway?"

When he'd lived with us, my father's studio had been the windowed storage shed at the foot of the driveway. He'd moved all the rakes, shovels, and household tools to one side, and set up an easel and drafting table on the other, although the table was always covered with junk mail and the only painting I ever saw on the easel was a birthday present for Ally, a green seahorse with one beach-glass eye, glued to the canvas. Up close, the glass was thinly scratched, luminous.

"If you look hard enough, you can see my name in there," Ally said, surprising me one afternoon when I was about to snoop through her closet. I peered closer, half hoping to see it and half wanting to tell Ally how dumb that was.

"I see it," I lied. "Alicia E. Foster."

"There's no e," she said.

Ally was nine. Once, she had been the one to pet strange dogs, brave the back of the school bus, and defy my parents' orders that we go to bed. Now she started wearing her Winnie the Pooh pajamas into the evening, when the three of us would settle around the television for dinner. Once, I found the pajamas—bright yellow, with Winnie's cheery, depressed smile aimed out at me—at the bottom of the stairs, heaped together with all the other laundry that never managed to get done. I took them by the sleeve and balled them into the space behind the dryer, but only ended up taking them out again before anyone knew. I was eleven years old and driven by guilt. There seemed to be no end of things you could feel guilty for. It was amazing. Sometimes, when I was paging through Ally's diary, I was sure someone was watching me from the doorway, disapproving. "I'm sorry," I'd say. "I'm so sorry."

Our mother worked as a telephone operator. Sometimes she'd work the late shift and we'd get a babysitter. Ally and I liked that. John was our favorite; talkative, assertive, full of silly voices, he liked to bring a telescoping chin-up bar that he braced high between the living room door jamb, raising Ally and me to it like we were part of a circus act.

"You're the man," he'd say, after I'd hung there for awhile, unable to lift myself more than an inch. "Think it. Know it. *Feel* it."

"The man," I'd stammer. My arms trembled, and my face grew hot, but I wanted to stay that way for a while. I wanted someone to take a picture of us together like that.

Sometimes we couldn't find a sitter. On those nights it was my job to look out after things. I'd jump whenever the phone rang—always my mother, on break, speaking to me through her headset, her voice both magnified and undersized, as if she were talking through a bottle. "I just had a guy ask me what the capital of Philadelphia was," she'd laugh, as I turned on the brass lamp beside my father's old fish tank, empty, bereft of pebbles. There was a light inside the tank and I turned that on, too, as I did the bedroom light, the bathroom light, and the diamond-shaped fixtures at the top of the stairs, the ones my father sometimes cleaned with a damp rag when Christmas rolled around, the ones that made the ceiling look like it was snowing electricity. "What did you tell him?" I'd say.

Later, I would find Ally asleep in front of the TV. She'd have her knees tucked up to her chin, a limp pillow across her lap, her thumb newly wet from sucking. The sight of her chewed nails made me want to shake her until the former Ally shook free, like I'd seen in the movies.

"Ally," I'd say, "snap out of it." Her eyes would flutter, wary of light.

"W-where am I?" she'd say.

"Home," I'd whisper.

"Home?"

I'd release my grip. She'd wipe a tear from her eye.

"Home," she'd say. "Oh—*home!*"

That spring two teenage boys were killed in a car crash just outside our neighborhood. They'd been drinking. Driving too fast. I knew the rest from the newspaper reports and local TV, knew that their names were Justin and Neil, that one had played soccer and the other had just won a scholarship to Penn, knew that their car had lifted off the road and struck a telephone pole so high up it must have been, as I overheard a teacher say, like a plane clipping a mountain. I knew that place in the road. A sudden rise that my father sometimes took too fast, on my request, when we were alone together and the only sound was the *do-lang-do-lang* of oldies radio and the air whistling through the passenger window. "Do the turn," I'd say, then slouch down and see the sky fatten above the dash, the effect like launching into space.

"Woo," my father would say.

"Woo," I'd say.

Sometimes, when my mother worked nights, I'd turn on all the downstairs lights and wash the dishes that no one seemed to wash anymore: Ally's milk glasses on the living room end table, my mother's coffee cups beside the microwave, pebbly with grounds and hard to scrub, and my peanut-butter toast plates, flecked with black crumbs that swirled around the kitchen drain and finally disappeared into the wherever beneath the sink. I liked washing the dishes. I liked having all the lights on. It put me at a kind of ease. I kept imagining a scene in my head where Justin and Neil showed up at our door, barely scratched, hungry for toast, and I fed them at the kitchen table on plates that glistened around the edges. "Wow," they'd whisper. "Now *that's* clean."

After a while we stopped bothering with sitters. "Randy tied up the phone for two hours," my mother would say, or "John never remembers messages," but Ally and I knew the truth: the house was a wreck; we didn't want anyone in. In. The opposite of out, where clothes dryers didn't break, leaving jeans and T-shirts to sag from kitchen chairs, where fireplaces weren't crammed with pizza boxes and flattened milk cartons, where Post-it notes— "Call about furnace!"—didn't go unread for weeks, lose their filmy grip and slip beneath the refrigerator that rocked each time the compressor kicked in. I spent my evenings watching TV with Ally, eating gooey maraschino cherries straight from the jar, or rectangles of baking chocolate we found in the back of the pantry, leftovers from the days of holiday parties and weekend guests. Ally's favorite was a drink she called Ruby Red—grenadine, tonic water, and the liquid from the bottom of the cherry jar—which she made especially in time for prime-time TV, where grown-ups fell in love on a tall cruise ship, played out their fantasies on a remote island, and shot a man in a ten-gallon hat over love.

At school it was rumored that our math teacher, Mrs. Harlan, was having an affair with Mr. Di Gregory, the softball coach.

"They were caught doing it in the locker room," people said. "Mr. Woods found them. That's why he quit," the rumor went, making several disparate parts fit, neatly, like a trombone into its case. "Because Mr. Woods was also doing it with Mrs. Harlan. He couldn't take it. Seeing them doing it like that. He broke down right there and cried. He's in therapy now. Last weekend someone saw him at the mall talking to the water fountain outside Nordstrom. He was tossing pennies in, muttering 'Bubbly, bubbly, bubbly.'"

I was in sixth grade and didn't know any girls. Once, my social studies teacher had said, "You know, if you cornered me in a dark alley and asked me to list all the state capitals for my life, I'd probably be dead." An idea that haunted me: *If you cornered me in a dark alley and asked me to introduce you to girls I knew, I'd probably be dead.*

I did know Janna, my father's new girlfriend, but that hardly seemed to count. Janna had been a student of his a few years back. She was in college now, splitting her time between my father's tiny, two-bedroom apartment and her duplex, which she shared with a blind man named Al, who, she said, could induce squirrels to climb on his shoulders, two and three at a time, simply by calling out, "Nut-a-cluck-cluck, nut-a-click-click."

"He thinks it's no big deal," Janna said.

We were watching movies in the small bedroom, where my father had pushed two sofas against the wall; at night these became beds for Ally and me. Janna was sitting next to me, her leg touching mine, while my father lay on the other sofa, his head propped by cushions; he and Janna made a show of not sitting together when we were around, as if Janna was a boarder whose name he could never quite remember. Ally sat beside me, sucking her thumb on the sly. "Sometimes I hear mice in this sofa," she whispered. "I think they've got a house in there."

"Actually, it's a school," Janna said. "For gifted mice. Micesourri. Maybe you've heard of it." She squeezed the cushion behind Ally's head. "Sometimes you can make the bells go off that way."

"Really?"

"Unless it's a holiday," Janna said. "Then what's the use?"

I looked at my father. I wanted him to say something. I wanted him to say, "There's no mice in the sofa, Ally. And there's no bells in the cushions, because I wouldn't let that kind of thing happen to the place where you two sleep. Understand?" But he didn't. He turned a smile on the two of them, and allowed his socked foot to touch Janna's leg. That day we'd gone to a petting zoo, where dirty goats chewed my shoelaces into a slimy pulp. I'd been so busy screwing my mouth into a smile I didn't even notice that I'd started to cry until I pushed my way into the men's restroom, where the mirrors afforded an embarrassing view of grandfathers shaking themselves before cascading urinals. I washed my hands like they were part of a game whose object was to get as much water on your fingers without rinsing the soap away.

"All day I've been thinking we should watch a movie together," my father said, "and here we are watching a movie together." He tapped the sofa armrest. "It's a lucky thing when you can have days like that. Makes you feel thankful. Appreciative."

"We had a blast," Janna said.

"Yeah," Ally said, forgetting the tantrum she'd thrown in the Dairy Queen parking lot when she saw yellow jackets spiraling above the trash cans.

"It was fun," I said.

"Because that's how I feel. Lucky," my father said. "Lucky to be together." He gave us an awkward smile, and for a moment I was afraid I was going to see my father cry. "All of us together like this."

Sometimes, when she was in a mood, my mother would say, "Your father always wants to think he's happy, even though he never is. Did you ever notice that about him?"

I said I didn't know.

"It's not hard to notice," she said. "Once you do, you can't stop noticing it."

When Janna came in to say goodnight, she'd tell us stories from her childhood. She'd grown up on a farm in rural Ohio. I liked to imagine Janna and me hanging out in a barn, where pigeons chuckled quietly from shadowy lofts. "Wow," I'd say, if it ever came to pass, "here we are in a barn."

"Yeah," Janna would say, "here we are."

"The two of us," I'd say, and then—what? What came next? "Sure is drafty in here?" *Sure is drafty in here!*

If Janna said goodnight to me last, I'd try to engage her in some conspiratorial conversation. "I'm worried about Ally," I'd whisper.

"Really? Why?"

"Did you see the way she freaked about those yellow jackets? She pulls stuff like that all the time now. I don't get it."

"We'll have to keep an eye out," Janna said. "That's for sure." She'd leave the bedroom door a little open, the way Ally liked it. In the semidarkness, I'd try to think of the saddest things I knew, a nighttime hobby of mine. I liked to feel a little chill, then pull the blankets around me, feeling warm and safe. I imagined myself riding along with Neil and Justin, telling them to slow down. I sat in back, windblown and panicked. "Please," I'd say, "I know something you don't." The two of them would ignore me, laughing, passing another Coors.

"I know something you don't," they'd laugh. "Oh, *I know something you don't.*"

The next time I saw Derek Trotter he was kicking holes in our deck. I was upstairs, camped beneath my bedsheets, my underwear to my ankles, paging through one of Ally's Nancy Drew mysteries. I had a thing for the illustrations. Whenever my mom and Ally were away I liked to take the books to bed with me and gradually remove my clothes, glancing through the illustrations, until I felt my heart beating in my ears. I liked the captions the best. "Don't move!" Nancy cautioned. "You're at the edge of the precipice!" I'd read them aloud, then feel suddenly embarrassed, closing the book and dressing in a matter of seconds.

"You ever heard of weatherproofing?" Derek said, when I opened the sliding glass door to the deck.

"Sort of?" I said.

"Yeah, you sort of heard of everything." He stomped his boot through another board. The board splintered and fell away, leaving a hole. "Jesus H. Someone could fall right through and break their fucking leg. Is that what you want? A lawsuit?"

"No," I said.

"Don't you know what a tort is?"

"What's a tort?"

"Well, it's a—well, goddammit, you can't have these boards all rotted out like this. Jesus!"

I stepped onto the deck and looked through a hole. Below, the part of the lawn I was afraid to mow, grass as high as my socks. It was late May, and I'd been out of school less than a week.

"We've gotta knock the rest out," Derek said, "before someone falls through." The logic of this suddenly arranged itself before me, plainly, like a vision.

"Okay," I said.

I watched Derek stomp the rotted boards with his heavy-heeled work boots. I had never noticed, until now, that Derek Trotter's left arm was shorter than the right. His left hand was undersized, too, with pale, knobby fingers and thick, uncut nails that trapped half-moons of dirt underneath. He was barely taller than me. Whenever he spoke, thin bands of saliva hinged the corners of his mouth. Watching him, it occurred to me that Derek Trotter must have been unpopular and lonely, an idea which filled me with a gray sort of kindliness toward him.

"What the fuck you looking at me like that for?" he said.

"Nothing," I said.

He put a finger to my chest. "Don't think I don't know that you're going to grow up faggy," he said. "Everybody knows."

I wanted to say, What do you mean everybody knows? but Derek slapped me on the head. "Now, get down there and pick up those boards."

"You hit me," I said.

"Ooh, I hit you," Derek said. "Maybe you hit yourself." He laughed. "Ever think of that?"

I stood beneath the deck, shaken. "I hate it down here," I said. Derek stood above, watching me through a hole. Light slanted in from the spaces where the deck no longer was.

"Maybe if you mowed the goddamned grass it wouldn't be so bad. It's a little thing called lawn care," Derek said.

"I saw a snake down here one time."

Derek stomped the board above my head. "You know what?" he said. "You're a little girl. Seriously. That grass is just grass, you dumbshit. It's like any other grass anyplace else."

Like any other, I thought as I stepped through, gathering the splintered boards in my arms. They were dry and brittle, with bent nails dangling from their ends. It occurred to me that my father had helped build this deck, that he might have put those nails in himself. When Derek descended the deck stairs, I slipped one of the nails into my jeans pocket.

"Put those in my trunk," he said.

I looked at him like he'd asked me my opinion of snowflakes.

"Now."

"It's the lack of a male influence," Derek said as I dumped the boards into the trunk. "Everybody knows that's what'll drive you faggy in the end." He laughed, wiped his nose. "*In the end.* God, that's good."

A few weeks later I would ride with him to Campfire Lake. We'd steal a paddleboat and paddle it to the center of the lake. The lake would be skinned with spring pollen and lily-white buds. I'd touch my hand to the water. But for now I stood in my driveway and tried to think of ways to explain what had happened to the deck.

"Tell them a dog did it," Derek said.

"A dog did it," I told my mother. We were standing in front of the sliding glass doors, open for the first truly hot day of summer.

"A dog?"

"He was huge," I said. "I heard him the other night when I was putting Ally to bed. She made me look outside because she thought it was a wolf. So I looked," I said, almost seeing it myself. "And there he was."

"And there he was," my mother said.

"Stomping his paws right through." Before Derek had closed the trunk, he'd lifted one of the splintered boards to his lips and tasted it with his tongue. "He was scary," I said.

I understood that my mother did not believe me, that she only felt guilty for being away at night when I might pursue some sort of mischief with all its attendant lies, but I did not want to understand that, so I allowed myself to think I had fooled her. The next few weeks when she left for work, I'd wait on our front porch for Derek Trotter. He'd slow the car in front of the house, not bothering with the driveway, as I ran to the door and opened its heavy latch with both hands. "Just like a puppy dog," Derek said, after I'd drawn my seatbelt across my chest.

Outside, neighborhood houses sped by like places in a dream.

The first time I rode with him, Derek pulled into a ritzy neighborhood a mile from the camp, then slowly patrolled all the cul-de-sacs, dead ends, and unmarked avenues, stopping wherever someone had left their trash. "Go check," he said.

"For what?"

"Pine."

"I'll get in trouble."

"Trouble for what?" Derek said. "Is there a law against taking trash?" This was one of Derek's favorite questions, and he used it often, as when we lit fires beside the lake (no, I couldn't exactly say I'd *heard* of a law against that) or stole sodas from the Pepsi machine inside the boathouse (in a way, they'd been *left* there for us, hadn't they?) or unchained the seagreen paddleboat that took us to the center of Campfire Lake (well, that's what a paddleboat was *for* anyway, wasn't it?).

That day we found a wooden patio chair, left out with the other garbage. "Holy shit," Derek whispered. "Tank is gonna go apeshit for that."

"Yeah," I said. "Apeshit."

Derek flicked his middle finger against my ear. "Don't curse to be cool. Makes you sound ignorant." My ear throbbed, and I felt tears in my eyes.

"But you said—"

"I said get that fucking chair," Derek said. "Now."

I lifted it into the trunk, hating Derek, wanting to tell him what an asshole he was—that was the word I would use, too, see how he liked it—but I didn't. Instead, I said, "It won't fit. The trunk can't close."

"Then hold it down," Derek said.

Right, I thought, gathering myself into the trunk, holding the hood against the chair. Inside, the scratchy carpet was slightly damp and malodorous but, as we pulled away, I saw the long windows of the showplace homes, felt the wind around my shoulders and knees, and it was like settling down into bed with the door partly open and Janna about to kiss me goodnight. I readjusted my legs and rocked with the motion of the car.

At one time Campfire Lake had been a real summer camp, with kids from the whole state traipsing in with mosquito netting, flashlights, and a vague ignorance of anything having to do with nature, but that was all years ago. Now it had become a ghost camp, rented out for occasional retreats and artist "colonies," quiet for months on end. We pulled into the gravel parking lot, where weeds jutted out from white rocks with the words W E L C O M E   C A M P E R S painted on in a joyless black script. From the parking lot, it was a slow climb up a marshy hill—this was my favorite, the swallows and nuthatches taking flight whenever the tackle box rattled—then the narrow passage beneath the waterfall where the top lake emptied into the second, smaller lake, a green pool with branches and logs floating on top. Sometimes Derek would stop by the largest log, where box turtles congregated, and push each off with the tip of his fishing rod. "Stupid turtles," he'd say. "Thinking they're the whole world."

My job, when we reached the upper lake, was to wade in to my knees and unlock the paddleboat we used to paddle to the center. Once there, we'd dump whatever pine we'd found: the chair, a bundle of boards, a tiny evergreen I'd had to hold with both arms while my feet strained against the pedals. Dumping the pines was Derek's idea. Our first trip out, he'd explained. "It's like this: Tank loves pine. Everybody knows it's his personal thing, right? He loves pine trees, pinecones, pinewood—shit, he'd probably get a boner for an air freshener. So I've been stacking them high, making a nice little pine house for him, and one day he's going to be sitting in it thinking, 'This is such a nice pine house. I hope I never have to leave.' And then he's going say, 'But what's with this toothache?' and that's when I'm going to say, 'That's my goddamned Mister Twister hooking your fat fucking lip, you piece-of-shit fish!'"

"It's like *On Golden Pond*," I said.

Derek glanced at me. "What's a golden pond?"

I explained the movie to him.

"Jesus. Is that the kind of shit you watch?" He spat a loogie into the water. "Sounds like a bitch flick to me."

My second job was to steal sodas from the ancient Pepsi machine in the boathouse. Derek liked to drink soda at all times, since, he explained, the carbonation helped cleanse your teeth and keep bad tastes away. He sometimes gargled with Mountain Dew while I watched, intrigued. "That's how Indians used to do it," he'd say, wiping his mouth. To help carry the sodas, Derek let me take his GripRite! fishing net, which had a magnificent green handle with the shiny GripRite! logo stuck above the rubber grip. When Derek was out of earshot, I liked to talk into the net like it was a microphone. "He's approaching the waterfall," I'd say, with a sportscaster's urgency. "Folks, looks like he's entered the boathouse in record time."

There was a girls bathroom inside the boathouse and sometimes I went in there to wash my hands and feel the thrill of being inside a forbidden place. Fishing bored me. I hated standing on shore all day while Derek paddled around in the boat, snagging and unsnagging his line from the glut of pines deep beneath the surface. When he got tired of drifting around he'd paddle in and cast from the shore, sticking his fishing rod in the flat apron of wet dirt that rimmed the lake. This seemed to go against the very idea of fishing itself, which I pointed out to him once as he slurped a Pepsi I'd nearly dropped on the walk back.

"Makes no difference," he said. "Hooks 'em just the same."

The day we dropped the patio chair in, we watched as it resisted sinking, steady above the water, defying all physics. Then the back legs tipped, suddenly, and the chair rocked back onto itself, like a kid accidentally dozing in Algebra. The water was murky, but I could just make out the legs slipping into the darkness. When it was gone, I could see the two of us reflected in the water's surface, eager, and a little in awe. "The water makes us look squiggly," I said.

Derek slapped my neck. "Stop saying shit like that," he said.

By August, my father and Janna had moved into a town house a few miles from the high school where my father's faculty yearbook photo showed his lips drawn into an implied smile, another doomed beard finding strange purchase along the boyish slope of his jaw. This year's caption was "Anybody got a paintbrush?!"

"*Anybody got a paintbrush?!*" Janna said. "Don't you think they could have come up with something better?" The four of us were unloading boxes of books in the middle of the curtainless living room. Ally and I had been distracted by a box of my father's old Bobbsey Twins books. On the flyleaf of each, my father's first attempts at self-portraits, an almond-eyed boy with grim lips and cropped hair.

"Oh, I don't pay any attention to those," my father said.

Janna tossed the yearbook aside. "Well, maybe you should," she said. "Maybe someone should take these kids aside and tell them they're not as clever as they think they are. I know I'd like to."

My father shrugged. "Not sure what good that'd do," he said. Beneath each portrait my father had included his name, address, and phone number, a habit that endured in all my school drawings. I liked the idea of someone finding them later on, wondering if they should call.

"God, I used to think I was *everything*," Janna said.

That night Janna tucked me in in my new room. My father had hung a sheet across the window, blocking out the streetlight that made clicking noises I'd thought were fingernails tapping the windowpane. It was the first time I'd ever been alone in a bedroom with Janna. "Sometimes I get freaked out by the streetlight," I said. She sat next to me, her hair still wet from a before-bed shower. "I wake up and think it's someone outside." Janna put a hand to my head and gently rubbed my hair.

"Sometimes everything seems freaky," she said.

Janna's body gave off a whiff of lavender and citrus. I balled my fists beneath the pillow and felt tears in my eyes. "Janna," I whispered.

"Hmm?"

"I heard those boys," I said. "The boys who died."

"You did?"

"I'm pretty sure. I mean, I heard something." I paused. "I've never told anyone before."

"That's okay," Janna said, but I couldn't tell what was supposed to be okay. The thing was, I wasn't really sure I'd heard the accident. I remembered putting Ally to bed, closing her door. I remembered turning on the hall lights and the lights outside. I heard a noise. A sound like a shopping cart slipping into another. I opened the front door and listened. I heard insects, a dog barking. A truck gearing down. I closed the door. "I think about it sometimes," I said.

"I'll bet," Janna said.

The next morning I found Ally in the bathroom, crying. "I don't know how to make it go," she said. She had the bathwater running, unable to figure out the shower. "You just press the brass button in," I said.

"*You* do it!" she cried. "I don't get it!"

"Ally," I said, "it's a shower like any other shower, and a button like any other button. Just press it, and the shower will turn on." I closed the door and listened to her sobbing. A moment later I heard the shower kick in. When I walked away I could hear Ally singing "Deck the Halls" in a voice I'd never noticed was lovely before.

"He's on to me," Derek said. We were picking lures from Derek's tackle box. "He's sick of everything I've got."

"This one's nice," I said, selecting a plastic minnow with two chandelier hooks hanging form each end. "I like the hooks."

"Saltwater lure," Derek said.

It was the end of August and I'd grown tired of the quest for Tank. Some days Derek would reel in a catfish and I would feel a flicker of excitement—at long last, the end—but these, according to Derek, were Tank's "bitches," and he'd toss them back. Other days Derek would catch sunfish, whose sharp dorsal fins always pricked him when he dislodged the hook, and throw them into the campfire I was allowed to stoke with dead branches and leaves. "Serves you right," Derek would say. "Burn in hell."

Derek found a lure, then ordered me to go get soda. When I returned, he cracked open a Mr. Pibb, then spat it out. "Jesus. This soda's piss-warm." He threw the can into the weeds. "Tastes like canned shit." I told him they must have just restocked the machine. Derek turned on me. "Don't you think I know that?"

he said. "You think you're smarter than me now? Some kind of soda expert?"

"No," I said.

"Mr. Pibb himself?"

"You shouldn't litter like that."

Derek grabbed me by my T-shirt and swung me to the ground. "You're a goddamned baby," he said. He kicked me in the side. "Now see if you can get us some cold sodas, Mr. Pibb."

I lingered in the girls bathroom. I locked the door and ran my hands under the sink. In the mirror, my eyes looked raw, red. I wiped my hands on my shorts and decided I would spend the rest of my life in the girls bathroom at Campfire Lake. I sat on a radiator and twirled the GripRite! between my feet, idly. I shouldn't have been surprised when Derek knocked, but I was. "I'm not coming out," I said.

"Don't be stupid," Derek said. "Open the door."

"I'm tired of you hitting me."

A moment later I heard Derek rattling the Pepsi machine. Then a metallic tapping against the bathroom door. "Listen," he said. *Tap, tap.* "You hear that? I got you a nice cold Pepsi. Now come on. Why don't you come out here and drink it? Okay?" *Tap.* "Doesn't that sound good? Mmm, that's refreshment."

"You take me for granted."

"Oh, *Christ.* What do you think you are, my *girlfriend*? 'You take me for granted.' That's funny."

"You're not really my friend."

Derek laughed. "You know what? You don't *have* any friends. Ever notice that? Unless we're counting your freaky little sister. Little Miss Freakface."

"At least she doesn't have to hang around with little kids just to feel big," I said.

Derek beat against the door. "Come on out and say that, shithead. Come on!"

I stood, but didn't walk to the door.

"Right. Didn't think so. You know what? You're a faggot," Derek said. "And that's all you'll ever be." I heard him lean against the door, putting his lips to the crack. "And by the way, that Pepsi was diet, so fuck you!"

I waited twenty minutes before opening the door. It was too far to walk home, plus I needed to get my socks and shoes from the lakeside, so I meandered along the smaller lake, knocking pebbles in with a swing of the GripRite!, deciding how to approach Derek. My plan: run if he came toward me. I was worrying about the details of my escape route when I noticed a gray fish moving just beneath the surface of green algae. He swam beside a log, and I recognized him as Tank the way I recognized my name in cursive. When I scooped him into the GripRite! one of his long whiskers lopped over the side of the net. He was heavy as a sack of rice.

"Derek," I said, when I'd gotten within earshot. "I've got something to show you."

Derek turned, knee-deep in the lake, negotiating a snag. "What? Your bra and panties?"

I'd had never known, until then, the feeling of winning—and winning big. Once, in third grade, I'd won a gift certificate for selling the most holiday candles (my mom ran a small operation out of her office), but it had been a long, tough drought ever since. I watched Derek step onshore and felt the triumph and regret peculiar to overdogs.

"No," I said. "It's your fucking fish." I hoisted the net in the air. Tank flapped inside, his thick tail writhing.

"Holy," Derek said.

I held the net over the water. "And he hates pine." Tank fell with a heavy plop, scaring up clouds of murky water. And then I felt blood on my tongue, felt Derek's bony knuckles against my face, head, side. I covered as best I could, but he was too much. "You goddamned piece of—" He landed punches on my arms and shoulders. I knew I was crying, but I wasn't ashamed. "It's not that bad," I said.

"Shut up!"

"It's not that bad at all."

When Derek left me, I lay on the ground for a while, feeling the blood pulsing in my temples.

There is one night that marks the end of that summer, although it was not the night I explained my cuts and bruises to my mother, not the night my father told Ally and me that he and Janna were getting engaged, not the night I stopped turning all the lights on. It was the night Ally and I heard a knock at the door, heavy, insistent. "Open up!" a voice said. "Please!"

I looked at Ally and felt my legs go rubbery. "Don't!" I hissed. "It's Derek." We were standing in the front foyer, Ally in her pajamas, me holding an iron fireplace poker, ready for Derek to break through, enraged.

"Please!" a female voice said. "We've been in an accident!"

When Ally opened the door, we saw a two teenagers, a boy in a leather jacket hugged to the chest of a blond-haired girl. There was blood down the boy's face. The girl held a blood-soaked newspaper to his eye. "We saw your lights," she said.

Ally led them to the kitchen, while I hid in the living room, afraid they were criminals. I couldn't stop my legs from shaking. I watched as Ally sat the girl down at the kitchen table, then led the boy to the sink. She turned the faucet on and held a damp dish towel to his eye.

"I'm so thirsty," the boy said. "You have no idea."

Ally took a cup from the drying rack and filled it with water. "This water is magic," she said.

"Magic water," the boy said. Ally held it to his lips.

"We hit a pole," the girl said. She began to cry. "My parents are going to kill me."

"I've never been so thirsty," the boy said. "This is the thirstiest I've ever been." He was stooped toward the sink, his ringed fingers gripping the countertop. Ally folded the towel against his eye. The fold clouded with blood. "We were driving," he explained.

He would lose that eye. I would know. I would see him, years later, when I entered state college, just miles from home. He would stand on street corners, a biker-boy with a studded jacket and mutton chops, a dramatic black patch over his left eye. A little mutt dog would trail at his feet, tethered to a public bench where kids with skateboards smoked inelegantly under the elms. He would heckle me for quarters.

But that night he stood against the sink, newly damaged, as Ally fed him cup after cup of tap water. "When we saw those lights," he said, "we knew this was home."

A Tiny Raft

That morning Reynolds went to the dentist, where his hygienist was a young woman whose son had recently shot a deer. A photograph of the boy leaning from the deer's antlers hung from a pegboard next to the office window, which looked out onto a parking lot just beginning to blanch with snow. "His very first deer," the hygienist said. "You should hear his father talk." Reynolds allowed her to vacuum the inside of his mouth with a white tube, whose opening, he noticed, was notched like a colander, and whose neck wore a slick patina of saliva and blood. He had always been something of a bleeder.

"We're expecting our first in April," Reynolds said. "It's a girl."

"Girls are easier," the hygienist said. "My second was a girl.

She's four now. Doesn't like to nap anymore, though. That's her latest thing. Says naps are boring."

"Ha," Reynolds said. The hygienist, up close, was older than Reynolds had first imagined. Faint lines around the eyes and a bagginess about the neck. Reynolds was thirty-nine; it embarrassed him to have put off children so long. "Boring."

"Oh, *everything's* boring. Naps, haircuts, church. Could you turn a little more toward me? Thanks. We're in our boring phase."

Yes, Reynolds thought, at least thirty-six, maybe thirty-seven. "We're in our worried one," Reynolds said.

"Your what?"

"Our worried phase."

"Oh," the hygienist said, but Reynolds sensed he shouldn't have said anything. As if to confirm his doubt, the hygienist asked him to close his mouth around the tube, which immediately drew his lips together and made a sound like an unstopped drain. A television had been mounted to the ceiling, tuned to CNN. Reynolds watched a helicopter circle above a floodplain, where bare trees rose from brown water, their branches asking, *What next?* The hygienist's tool made a whirring noise and gave off a whiff of rubber. All these new older parents, Reynolds thought, pushing forty, tricking time. His own mother had had him when she was nineteen.

"What sort of work do you do?" asked the hygienist.

"I'm a teacher," Reynolds said. "High school math and social studies." He neglected to mention drama. This year they were doing *Don't Drink the Water*. Reynolds had pushed for *The Seagull*.

"Oh, math was never my thing," the hygienist said. "You'd laugh if you heard my grades."

"Not at all," Reynolds said.

"But you would. Could you tilt your head just a little? Better."

"Almost everyone feels that way," Reynolds said.

"Do they?"

"Sure," Reynolds said, but it sounded more like *sore*. The hygienist put the tube between his lips. "Close, please," she said. "There we go. No, I think I'm more of a creative person. I like making things with my hands. Painting, pottery, needlepoint.

Things like that. Last May my girlfriends and I took a trip to colonial Williamsburg and I couldn't believe all the things those people could do with their hands. I said to my friend, 'I'd like to be like that.' Handy, you know."

"Candles," Reynolds said.

"Right."

"I'd like to make a table."

"Apple butter," the hygienist said.

A moment later the doctor appeared. A ruddy face pinched by bifocals whose safety lenses were flipped up. Breath like peppermint tea. "So, this is the guy who brought the snow?" he said.

"Could be," the hygienist said.

Reynolds made a "who me?" face. For as long as he could remember, people treated him like someone much younger than he actually was. A part of himself dwelled happily within this misunderstanding, but more and more Reynolds felt he was committing a fraud. The doctor shook his hand and explained that Reynolds had one small cavity—a "pipsqueak"—that might be wise to fill. Reynolds assented by giving a thumbs up.

"What I like to hear," the doctor said.

Reynolds's sense of the procedure was threefold. The doctor's gaze, illuminated by a bright lamp whose center bore a blue oval like a sunspot; the television, where a commercial showed a house dressing itself in Tyvek siding, slipping it on like a dinner jacket; and the snow falling on bare trees outside. Trees were everywhere, Reynolds thought. He had the nicest tree outside his office, whose longest branch sometimes delivered fat cardinals to his window. He'd once tried writing a poem about it, but felt embarrassed afterward, and saved the poem to his Misc. Expenses folder. Sometimes, while teaching, Reynolds had an urge to recite lines from this poem. He had a reputation as a teacher who could be made to blush.

"I'm just jiggling your cheek to get the Novocaine flowing," the doctor said. "A little jiggle goes a long way, I always say."

A golfer, Reynolds thought.

As he was filling the cavity, the doctor said, "I don't suppose you have a student named Timothy Weston?"

"Westbourne," the hygienist said.

"That's right. Westbourne."

Reynolds, with a slight shake of his head, indicated no.

"Well, this kid comes in here about two, I guess it was maybe three months ago, says he wants to speak to 'the doctor of the house.' Wouldn't talk to anybody else. Sat in the waiting room for over an hour and waited for me while I was in the middle of an extraction. A whole hour. Anyway, I try to be friendly, say 'What can I do for you today?' and this kid just stares at me, I mean *stares*"—the doctor gave Reynolds a look.

"Right," Reynolds said.

"Says, 'Do you realize that one in three Americans eats less than one serving of citrus fruit a week?' Turns out this kid is selling grapefruit for his school marching band. He's got a whole stack of brochures and order forms in his book bag. They need the money to go to Disneyworld." The doctor laughed.

"Right," Reynolds said.

"But here's the best part. The kid wants *me* to sell the grapefruit *for* him. Says I could pitch it as a kind of alternative to sweet snacks. He's willing to give me a slice of the profit. I say, 'Tell you what, I'll pass your brochure around the office, see if anyone's interested, but that's it.' I figured it was the least I could do. I mean, you have to kind of admire a kid like that."

"Sure," Reynolds said, now realizing that he knew the kid after all. Tim Warren. A former drama student who had once disrupted rehearsal by endlessly playing a single note on an upright piano until Reynolds asked him to cut it out. "There's angels inside this key," Tim had said.

"Long story short," the doctor said. "We end up buying nearly a hundred dollars of grapefruit, the kid collects the money, then—we never see the fruit. We've called the school, but they say they don't have anyone by that name. So what can we do, right?"

"Right."

"Still, what a character. Takes a few to make the world go round."

Reynolds could see his mouth in the reflection of the doctor's safety lenses. A halved strawberry nurturing a pink-gray tongue. Reynolds wondered if the doctor had affairs.

"You'll be a little numb for a while afterward, but not long," the hygienist said, when she escorted Reynolds to the cashier.

Reynolds nodded. Already he could feel the Novocaine wearing away—or was that a trick of standing up? "Thanks," he said.

"Keep up with the flossing," she said. "That'll help reduce some of your bleeding."

Some of your bleeding, Reynolds thought. The idea of a dentist's office seemed suddenly absurd to him. The way he'd felt as a kid, when, asked to take a nap on a bath towel spread across the backseat of his father's station wagon, the proximity of his unsleepy head to the road rushing beneath the car's tires made him newly aware that a car was truly an arrangement of soft chairs and conjoined seats asked, over and over again, to hurl through space at alarming speeds.

"And these are for you," the hygienist said, and handed Reynolds a miniature tube of toothpaste, dental floss, and green toothbrush. Reynolds accepted these gifts as part of a transaction where the queer intimacy of peering into a decaying mouth was quietly apologized for: he hadn't had this floss, this brush. He grabbed his coat from a waiting room chair and headed out to the parking lot, where snow was falling more heavily now, fat flakes clinging to his lapel. Those poor Ohio saps, Reynolds thought. He started his car and pulled out onto the highway, deserted at this time of day. The new filling thrilled the side of his tongue not affected by the Novocaine: it traveled there, exploring. When Reynolds had first had his braces removed, it took months for his tongue to stop calling on the backside of a molar that always held the flavor of soda, it seemed, no matter how well Reynolds cleaned. At a traffic light, Reynolds opened the toothbrush. When had toothbrushes become so scientific looking? This one had a curved head, an accordion neck, and bristles cut to three different lengths. It wasn't until Reynolds held it to the light that he realized the hygienist had given him a child's brush. A dinosaur smiled from inside its handle.

Home, Reynolds found Kathryn watching *The Price Is Right*. It was a new thing with her, daytime television. For years they'd neglected TV, only to find it just as they'd left it, which was a comfort, as was *The Price Is Right* theme music, recalling, to

Reynold's mind, mac and cheese, refrigerator magnets, and the sound his snow-boot laces made when, asked to separate from a frozen knot, stiffly complied.

"Don't get snow on the ottoman," Kathryn said.

"I won't."

"Leave your shoes on the mat."

"I saw two accidents on the way home," Reynolds said. "Both times the drivers stayed in their cars, talking on cell phones. Didn't even get out to check the damage." Reynolds flung his hat onto the magazine rack. "It's getting so you can't even get into a proper accident anymore."

Kathryn ignored him. She pulled an afghan pulled around her knees, and the afghan, too, was a reminder of the times Reynolds and his sister Meg would hide beneath the green-and-purple one that draped their family room sofa, peering out from yarny holes. They'd called this game "Outer Space."

"Did you take your vitamin?" Reynolds asked.

Kathryn checked her watch. "Not time yet."

"Did I ever tell you I used to be afraid of swallowing pills? Used to drive my dad nuts. He made me practice with Tic-Tacs."

Kathryn kept her eyes on the screen, where Bob Barker was pulling the third strike on Three Strikes. "No, I don't think you ever told me that."

"He'd say, 'Imagine the pill as a tiny raft going over an enormous waterfall. It wants to be swept along,'" Reynolds said. He hoped this would trigger Kathryn's memory of the first time he'd told her this story, back when they were first dating. It bothered him that she didn't remember.

"A tiny raft," Kathryn said. "Sounds like your dad."

"I still think about it every time I swallow a pill," Reynolds said. "Always."

"I'll have to try that," Kathryn said. She was ten years younger than Reynolds. Sometimes Reynolds wondered if he'd made a mistake. But didn't everyone think that sometime? Reynolds, wishing to ease the thought away, sat next to Kathryn and rubbed her feet. "They shot me full of Novocaine," he said.

"Poor baby," Kathryn said. She kissed his forehead. "My numb hubby."

"And I found out one of my former students is a grapefruit-scam artist."

"All in the same day," Kathryn said.

Reynolds told her the story. It made him feel good, telling it. He liked the way he hadn't said anything to the dentist about knowing the kid. That was the kind of person he was, he thought. Loyal. The hardest secret for a man to keep is his opinion of himself—where had Reynolds read that?

"I did something like that once," Kathryn said. "When I was in Girl Scouts. We were supposed to sell these doorstops shaped like caterpillars. Or was it snakes? No, it must have been caterpillars. Who would want a snake doorstop? Anyway, I made up all these phony orders and ended up winning a hair dryer. A very big deal for me. My very own hair dryer. I remember just standing in the bathroom, looking at it. I think it was the first thing I'd ever won. Anyway, when our troop leader found out what I'd done, she made me apologize to everyone in our troop. Individually. She had everyone stand in a circle holding these little white candles while I went around with a lit one, saying 'I'm truly sorry for what I've done.' When they said 'I forgive you,' I lit their candles." Kathryn looked at Reynolds. "You know what? That was one of the best times I ever had."

Reynolds put a hand on her shoulder. "I forgive you," he said, but Kathryn didn't say anything. On-screen, a contestant spun the wheel for the first Showcase Showdown. It heartened Reynolds to hear that they hadn't changed the sound the wheel made, a vague electronic slapping that slowed to a single beat. The contestant elected to spin again with seventy cents. *Mistake*, Reynolds thought.

"We got a package today," Kathryn said.

"Oh?"

"But they delivered it across the street."

"Hmm."

"We got a call from the Blackwells. They're holding it for us."

"The Blackwells?"

"The house across the street," Kathryn said.

"The trampoline house?"

Kathryn nodded. "Would you mind going over to get it? I think it's from my mother."

The request bothered Reynolds. "I'm not going to any trampoline house," he said. The trampoline was a joke between the two of them. On evening walks they'd dare each other to take a hop on it whenever the Blackwell girl wasn't around. The girl, nine or ten or eleven or twelve—who could tell with all that extra weight?—jumped on the trampoline with the practiced boredom of a tollbooth collector. "The whole house is probably built on springs and wires."

"Don't make this into something," Kathryn said.

"I'm not making this into something."

"You know what you're doing," Kathryn said, and flipped the page of a magazine.

Reynolds said, "Did you know that one in three Americans eats less than one serving of citrus fruit a week?"

"The package is probably something for the baby," Kathryn said.

"Isn't that bad luck?" Reynolds said. "Getting baby gifts this early?"

Kathryn didn't say anything.

"I've heard that's bad luck," Reynolds said.

———

The snow falling across the front yard lifted Reynolds' mood and lent his errand a feeling of escape. The street not yet sullied by plows! Reynolds pulled his scarf to his chin and rehearsed what he would say when the Blackwells answered the door. As a kid, he'd loved the way snow hid the neighborhood driveways, walkways, flower gardens, and property lines, whose borders seemed as real and substantial as the fences that sometimes separated them. Thrilling to walk across the front yard his father forbade him, in spring, to play upon; to hop the hidden curb whose storm drain he'd always been a little afraid of; to breach his neighbor's hedge like passing through an automatic door. "My wife says we got a call from you," he'd say. "About a package? Sorry to bother." Reynolds liked the picture of himself on the Blackwells' porch, his knit cap flecked with snow. As a kid, he'd liked kicking his boots against the doorstep. Take those things off and get yourself warm, the Blackwells might say.

The trampoline was covered with snow. A child's bike had been left on top, its handlebars turned the wrong way. Reynolds thought of the dead deer's antlers. At least he wouldn't have to go hunting, not with a daughter. Girls are easier. The ground underneath the trampoline was a neat circle of brown grass. Nice place to hide, Reynolds thought. Maybe they'd left the package between the storm and front doors.

No one answered his knock. A gauzy curtain limited his view, but Reynolds could see a room with a sofa and TV. The TV was an old console job, the kind he'd grown up with and sometimes missed. Kathryn said she could not remember a time before cable. This depressed Reynolds, whose job it had been to adjust the rabbit ears during football games when his grandfather pointed to the set. Up close, the TV gave off a warm kind of smell. Whatever happened to that smell? Reynolds pressed the Blackwells' doorbell. It refused to sound.

There were tire tracks leading to the garage and sets of footprints trailing off toward the back of the house. Reynolds followed them to a basement door, which held a diamond-shaped window, lit from the inside. The window afforded a view of a bare lightbulb whose string juddered as if caught in a breeze. Stepping closer, Reynolds saw a man and a young girl—the trampoline girl—playing Ping-Pong. The man hit an easy serve, which the girl missed by feet. A small radio sat atop the table, clearly in the field of play. The girl held her paddle like it was a frying pan, so late were her swings. Before Reynolds backed away from the window, he saw her duck underneath the table to retrieve another missed return. The stepping away asked a question of him: Had the Ping-Pong table been painted bright red? The man's hair was matted with sweat.

If I go, I'll have to go home, and I don't want to go home, so I'll go, but not home, Reynolds thought. He was about to take a walk around the neighborhood—maybe their game would be over by then—when he saw the girl watching him through the basement window. She tapped the paddle against the pane. "Daddy!" she said. A moment later the door swung open, revealing the man, the Ping-Pong table, and the girl cowering underneath it.

"You scared my Gretchen," the man said. He had an accent

Reynolds couldn't place. "Gretchen, it's just the man from across the street. Won't you come out?"

"I'm sorry," Reynolds said. "I'm just here to pick up a package."

"This is a nice man," the man said. He introduced himself to Reynolds. Pavo. "This is the man who pulls his trash cans in a sled." The man winked at Reynolds. "Isn't that nice of him?" Reynolds had fashioned a trash cart out of plywood and lawn-mower wheels, trying, poorly, to imitate the one his grandparents had allowed him drag to the end of their driveway during summer visits. He'd gotten rid of it months ago. "We said that was nice of him, remember?" Gretchen crawled out and stood behind her father as if Reynolds might strike her. She wore butterfly barrettes. "Let's get this man warmed up."

The Ping-Pong table was bright red. Reynolds had been right about that. What he hadn't seen until now was that the table was actually two tables of different sizes clamped together by a net that seemed unnaturally high. The larger table put Gretchen at a terrible disadvantage. Freshman year, Reynolds had been the Ping-Pong champion of his dorm. "That's some Ping-Pong table," Reynolds said.

"Isn't it? Thank you. We made it, together. Didn't we, Gretchen?"

Gretchen sighed and pulled on her father's belt loop. "No," she said.

"But I bet you helped," Reynolds offered. "Painting it."

Gretchen hid again. "Daddy," she said.

"She gets nervous," her father said.

The basement ceiling was low. The lightbulb revealed bent nails hugging wooden beams, a spiderweb bannered between two gray pipes.

"Gretchen will get you your package," Pavo said.

"Great," Reynolds said. "Sorry again to bother."

"This man says sorry too much, doesn't he?"

"No," Gretchen said.

"Gretchen, the package."

While Gretchen ran upstairs, Pavo turned the radio down and told Reynolds the story of the Ping-Pong table. Reynolds listened, saying "wow" every now and then, or "sure." Sometimes

Reynolds wondered if people could tell how little he was paying attention to them. His students always gave him high evaluations for attentiveness and willingness to listen. This depressed him.

"Do you like this music?" Pavo asked.

The radio played classical music. "Yes," Reynolds said. "Very much." For a while Reynolds had tried to like classical music, but it always made him feel a little lonely. Kathryn had played violin as a child, and sometimes listened to Bach while washing dishes. This made Reynolds feel they were strangers. "But I don't know that much about it."

"What's to know?" Pavo said. He made a conducting motion. "Ah, the best part."

Reynolds nodded. He didn't like people spilling themselves all sloshy all at once. Pavo closed his eyes and brought the music to a close. "We used to go to concerts, my wife and I," he said. "We used to read books. We used to go to the theater. We used to—but, oh well."

"Things change," Reynolds said.

"Everything does."

Upstairs, they heard Gretchen dragging her feet. What could take this long?

"Would you like to play?" Pavo asked. He gestured toward the table. "Or do you not know that much about it?" He gave Reynolds a look.

"No, I'd be glad to," Reynolds said.

"Just until Gretchen gets back."

"Right." Reynolds took the larger end of the table while Pavo moved the radio out of the way. It felt good to have a Ping-Pong paddle in his hands again. The last time he'd played was at a faculty party, where he'd played badly, self-conscious about the V of sweat showing through his button-down shirt, afraid that winning might disturb the notion others had of him, if they had one at all. What did they think of him? They thought he was a little snobby and aloof—they resented his advanced degree, Reynolds was sure of that—but otherwise okay. Sometimes Reynolds imagined someone saying this about him, after he'd left the room. He liked the idea of someone listing his faults, then shrugging. "But he's okay," they'd say. "Otherwise."

Pavo opened with a lollipop of a serve, which Reynolds treated in kind. They volleyed for a while, feeling each other out. "We are too nice, right?" Pavo said, stroking a decent backspin. Reynolds returned it to the corner and got the return he wanted: rushed, placed too high, offering itself up for a smash. But Reynolds held back and ended up lobbing it into the net. "Aha," Pavo said. "One serving nothing." He held out his hand; Reynolds scooped the ball to him. "We'll play to eleven?"

"Eleven's fine," Reynolds said.

"Eleven's for us."

But at game point, Reynolds tapped a soft return, drawing Pavo to the net. There was a moment when Reynolds read Pavo's eyes, the surprising fear there, then sent Pavo's return where he'd had in mind all along: the back weak-side corner. The ball dinged off the table and went sputtering into the hot water heater. "Eleven serving eight," Pavo said, retrieving the ball. His forehead was damp with sweat. "No more kidding around, right?"

"Sure."

"Pavo, think!" Pavo said. "Concentrate." Reynolds tried a trickier serve, but Pavo's return caught Reynolds around the wrist. "See? You can do it, Pavo."

At ten serving fourteen, Gretchen reappeared. She sat on the basement steps, combing the hair of a plastic pony. "Gretchen, your father is losing," Pavo said. He winked at Reynolds. "Can you believe that?"

Gretchen touched the horse's nose to hers and made whinnying noises.

"Do you know what his secret is?" Pavo said. "He lets me make my own mistakes."

Reynolds didn't say anything. That *was* his secret.

"You could learn a lot from this man."

Gretchen whispered something to the pony. Reynolds wondered if she'd forgotten about the package. "I really should be getting back," he said.

"Gretchen, where is this man's package?"

Gretchen shrugged.

"Please find it. Now!" Pavo said. He struck the table with the paddle. Gretchen cradled the pony to her chest, but did not move. "Do as I say!" Pavo said.

"Oh, it's okay," Reynolds said. Gretchen began to whimper.

For a moment Reynolds wanted to make Gretchen cry. "Not a big deal. No problem."

"You could learn a lot from this man," Pavo said. "Discipline. Strategy." Pavo indicated that he was about to serve. "Knowledge," he said. "Technique." They began to volley. Pavo tightened his mouth, eyes narrowed. The expression reminded Reynolds of the occasion, a few months before, when he'd seen Pavo giving Gretchen a joyride atop the family minivan. Reynolds had motioned Kathryn over to the window, where she caught a glimpse of Gretchen hopping off the van's hood as Pavo rolled up the driver's side window. "You've got to be kidding me," Kathryn whispered.

They played to a tie, twenty-twenty. Reynolds had had opportunities to put the game away, but didn't. The sight of Pavo with his undershirt sticking to his chest, his face pink as a sliced melon, held him at bay. Twice, he'd had an opportunity to spike, but ended up floating both shots off the end of the table. "You're letting me back," Pavo said. "You know that, right?"

"Too many mistakes," Reynolds said.

"Too many presents," Pavo said. He prepared to serve. "Pavo, think," he said. "Don't let this man allow you to get ahead of yourself. That's his game." They volleyed for a while, until the basement door opened and Gretchen clopped down the stairs, a cardboard box under one arm. She stood in front of the hot water heater, sucking her thumb. The package was book-sized, probably not a gift from Kathryn's mother, Reynolds thought. The remembrance of what it was surprised him, as did his final shot, an easy lob that Pavo drilled into the away corner of the table.

"Game point," Reynolds said.

"You're embarrassing us," Pavo said. "Really. Please, do us a favor and not let me win, okay?"

Reynolds said he'd see what he could do, then served. Pavo returned his shot with a slight backspin that caught Reynolds off guard—his shot one-hopped over the net. "Damn," Reynolds said. He laid his paddle on the table. "Good game."

When he looked up, Pavo was holding the ball, lining up to serve. "Gretchen," he said, "this is a mean man. This is a mean man in our basement."

Gretchen looked at Reynolds, then ducked her head when he

tried to smile. "Well, I should probably let you two get back to your game," Reynolds said.

"Come here, Gretchen," Pavo said.

Gretchen shook her head.

"Now."

Gretchen set the package on the ground, but didn't move.

"You will play this man. He can teach you something."

"Oh, no, that's okay, really," Reynolds said. "I'm not much of a teacher." He stood away from the table, but already Pavo was dragging Gretchen closer, placing the paddle in her hand like it was a gun she didn't wish to handle. Reynolds saw that there was no way out.

"I want you to think," Pavo said, standing behind her. "I want you to think about what you're doing. Stop moping around. Stand straight. How can you play without standing straight?"

Gretchen sighed.

"This man will serve. He's good. But he will let you win. What do you think of that?"

Reynolds hit a few moderate serves, but Gretchen only clipped one of them, sending the ball up into the rafters, where it rattled around like a pinball, then fell out of play.

"Better," Pavo said, "but not good."

Gretchen rolled her eyes. "Who *cares*?" she mumbled.

"That's right. You don't care." Pavo looked at Reynolds. "Did you hear that? That's the way her friends talk. See what you've got to look forward to?"

Of course, Reynolds thought. Of course Pavo had seen Kathryn and him walking by. He'd seen them stop in front of trampoline, Kathryn's belly just beginning to show.

"It's a girl," Reynolds said.

"Hear that?" Pavo said. "You're playing a father."

Reynolds stroked a few softies across the net, which Gretchen managed to return. Her loose grip angled them toward the ceiling, where they hung for what seemed too long a time, sometimes catching the lightbulb's string.

"We've seen you, outside," Pavo explained. "Congratulations."

"Thanks," Reynolds said.

"Keep your shots down, Gretchen. Don't you know this man could put those away? Don't you know he's just teasing you?"

Gretchen's face, which always looked as if she had just sneezed, gave way to tears.

"This is the meanest man in the world. A teaser."

Gretchen lobbed another toward the ceiling. "Oh, *Daddy*!" she said, and her mouth crinkled into a cry. This mouth, a wet, needy thing, the last thing Reynolds remembered before he reached in to spike and smashed the lightbulb into a thousand pieces.

Pool Season

I remember a candy called Michigan Cherries. Dropped from machines with long knobs like pinball plungers, scooped from a narrow trough, the cherries arrived cracked, broken, weeping their pink centers. The centers had a faintly bitter taste—this, it seems to me now, was why Michigan Cherries were unpopular, along with their dull, window-envelope packaging—that lingered even after you'd rinsed with 7-Up and accidentally swallowed a few gulpfuls of pool water. Michigan Cherries were vended at the community pool.

My brother and I used to go to the pool together. Darren, sixteen, newly broad-shouldered, wearer of headphones, magnificently freckled, would drag a deck chair beneath a wide umbrella and prop his feet on my lounger, which creaked when he moved his weight. "This pool is so stupid," he'd say, then clap a cassette into his Walkman. "I mean, just *look* at it."

I looked. Mothers, grouped in twos and threes, kicking their feet in the shallow end, while their children navigated the U-shaped pole that sloped into the kiddie pool, their arms cartoonishly muscled with water wings. The same white-haired man I'd seen all summer long, swimming the margin of water between the deep-end ropes and the lifeguard post, his expression like he was choosing between brands of shoelaces. The fat girl still reading *The Thorn Birds*.

"No one even comes here anymore," Darren said.

"We do," I said, lamely. I was eleven and in love with the pool. The week before I'd found $1.60 in the teeth of the deep-end drain.

"Lucky us." Darren draped a T-shirt over his head. "If anyone needs me," he said, "I'll be in my sleeve."

That summer Darren moved in with our mother, who lived in the college town just miles from my father. They'd separated years before but had never gotten around to a divorce, a fact I carried around with me like the slim penlight in my book bag, emblazoned with the university logo on its cap. Our mother taught political science. I lived with my father, sleeping in Darren's old room. At night, I shone the penlight on the ceiling where Darren and my mom had once painted a whale mural, a gray humpback cresting through a high wave. The mural was gone now, but with the penlight you could still see the whale's jaw, ribbed like an umbrella.

Sometimes, when I got tired of searching for coins, I'd swim near the mothers, pretending to dive for a plastic tyrannosaurus I'd found in the kiddie pool skimmer. I kept him because some kid had painted teeth over the ones already there, which made him look abjectly sentient, like a blowfish or a team mascot. I'd toss him near the mothers, Rex disappearing with a toothy *plip!*, then swim beneath babies bobbing in Styrofoam triangles, pulled along by ropes attached to phantom hands, slender, and brightly nailed. Surfacing, the mothers spotted me, but spoke as if I wasn't there.

"You've got tell him that, Meg. I know how hard that's going to be, but you've *got* to do it."

"I know. It's just that I keep—hold on. Jason, *no*! That's not yours, okay? We don't take things that aren't ours. *Jason*! When we get home, you're having room time. Do you hear me? You're going room-room."

These conversations lingered as I pushed myself out of the shallow end and wet-walked to the vending machines, my feet trailing leaf-shaped prints that diminished to semicolons by the time I arrived back at the umbrella, where Darren was watching kids cannonballing from the high dive. "The fun's thinking you'll splash the lifeguards," he said, allowing me to pour Michigan Cherries into his cupped hand, "but you never really do." There was a spot above his right temple that trembled when he chewed; whenever I want to think of Darren, of pool season, that's the first thing I go for. I took a seat next to him. We shared the cherries. Darren is the only other person I can remember liking them. The day I found $1.60 in the deep end, I bought us each a bag.

When Darren was a baby he'd crawl into the tiniest spaces, eluding babysitters, aunts, parents. He'd escape his crib and wind up in the lee of a flipped wheelbarrow, or stretched behind the family room sofa, like a sunned cat. "We could always hear you," my mother would say, after cheerless holiday meals, conversation materializing too late, like the family Polaroid we'd finally re-member to take while dinner plates soaked in the kitchen and my father had already disappeared to his office. "That was the thing," she said. "You always called for us."

"I was thoughtful that way," Darren said, sipping egg nog from a squat glass. "Making it interesting for you."

"What did he say?" I asked, feeling I was keeping a volleyball in play.

"He said, 'Here's baby! Here's baby!'"

Darren laughed. "Here's baby," he said. "That's good. I'm going to start saying that again."

My mother took a sip of wine. "But who would be looking for you?"

A silence, suddenly arrived, like a flung snowball.

"I am," I said. "I mean, I would."

Darren looked at my mother; she trailed a bread heel across her plate. The two of them laughed. "Hear that?" Darren said. "Tim's looking."

The summer I'm thinking of, the one where the pool appears with weeds reaching through the chain link fence, with algaed scum slicking the men's shower floors, with the feeling, nearly inexpressible to me now, of hearing my name called as I surfaced from a dive, was the same summer Darren had a girlfriend, Mira. I remember her as pretty, dark-haired, prone to silent laughs that always made me a little bit uncomfortable, the three of us trapped at the end of a picnic table or pressed between the bucket seats of Darren's coupe, the one with the air conditioning that never worked quite right. She would cup a hand to her mouth, her eyes watering at the edges, and playfully punch Darren in the arm. This recalled gesture, boyish, brotherly, informs me that I was secretly in love with her, an embarrassment to me then.

"Hey, Tim," Darren said, turning his head to me, on a sweltering, afternoon drive. "Mira and I are going to a party this Friday and we were wondering how much money we'll need to buy some coke." Laughs. Mira's fist against his shoulder.

"Don't," she laughed, in a way that meant just the opposite. "You're mean."

"Who's mean? I just want to know how much money Tim thinks a little coke will cost."

I leaned forward. "I get the joke, you guys. Ha-ha."

"What joke?" Darren said. "I asked a simple question: How much money will we need for coke?"

"You want me to say it like it's drugs."

"I just asked a question."

"I'm not," the words *a little kid* passed in and out of possibility like swift geese, "an idiot."

"Who said you were an idiot? Did I say anyone was an idiot? Did I?"

"This is so mean," Mira said.

"Just tell me. How much money will we need for coke?"

I saw Darren's expression in the rear-view mirror, the pleased tension of his lips, and glimpsed, for the first time, the benign cruelty that attends all brotherly enterprise, the slapped pencil on a take-home quiz, the hard pitch to an ungloved hand.

"I don't know," I said. "I guess maybe two dollars."

Darren punched the steering wheel, laughing. "Two dollars! Oh, Jesus. *Two dollars!*"

Mira hugged her arms to her chest. "Oh, sorry," she laughed. "Sorry, Tim, sorry."

Sometimes the pool mothers would take laps during adult swim. I always liked it when that happened. I'd hang out in the kiddie pool and watch them, me with my knees to my chest, squatting to kiddie height, delighted I could still get away with that. The mothers would wait until all the kids cleared out and a row of lane markers was strung from the deep end to the shallow: the pool, seen from my vantage, an abacus tipped on its side. Before they dunked their heads, the mothers would remove their sunglasses, leaving them like black crabs on the rim of the shallow end. They'd swim in long, slow strokes, turning their heads left, right. Then they'd climb up onto the rim again, chatting, making jokes I couldn't hear. They'd find their sunglasses and slip them back over their ears. It always disappointed me to see them putting them on again.

Our mother, a New Yorker, had never learned to swim or drive a car, which had always irritated and fascinated me, since I was old enough to swim but not old enough to drive. Trips to grocery stores, birthday parties, and shopping malls were ordeals by public transportation, Darren, my mother, and me riding the too-clean transit bus through the suburbs, the world outside painstakingly arranged for milkshakes to be delivered through rolled windows, dog food to be heaved across trunked spare tires, and classmates to be dropped off at the curb, saying "See you on Monday." Inside, the bus smelled like new erasers and sliced lemons.

"Everywhere you look in this town it's like you're seeing it from behind," Darren said on one of these excursions, my mother smiling, suppressing a laugh. Darren hated the house our father had chosen nearly as much as our mother, and their shared grievance was a divide between Darren and me, as real and substantial as the wall that separated our bedrooms, mine tacked with posters of wildlife, Darren's with models, rock stars, Jackson Pollock squinting behind a dangling cigarette. I looked outside, wanting to defend the row homes with awnings rolled against their mounts, whose facades had always reminded me of cats waking from naps. I wanted to say how remarkable it was that we could hear the town waterfall at night, always there, until I realized that was something my father would say. Instead, I said, "This bus is one fucking clean machine," and the two of them laughed, the divide momentarily lowered, a hopped net.

My mother kept a guitar in her home office, an acoustic with a thick strap. Sometimes I'd pick it up and try to strum a little something, but I could never remember the chords my mother had shown me, on summer afternoons when I'd wandered into her office, my mom two-finger typing at her IBM Selectric, whose round, juddering ball fascinated me with its insistent march across the page, onionskin paper curling out the top like a scissored ribbon. She was a poor typist, but beautiful and funny, a whisperer of private jokes, and this made the clumsiness of her typing seem somehow superior to me than actual typing. "Two thoughts for a happy life," she said, hearing me in the doorway. "One: don't go into academia, and two: don't get married." She spun around to face me. "Don't look so worried, Tim. I'm just kidding." She reached for the guitar and motioned me closer. "You can go into academia if you want."

My father was a lawyer. His home office was next to the laundry room, tiny, spare, decorated with the calendars Darren and I invariably bought him each Christmas. On his desk he kept a stuffed Kermit the Frog doll my mother had given him when they were first living together. My father, shy, terrified of public speaking, had used the doll to get through his first year of litigation, practicing his spiel on thoughtful, receptive Kermit, his cartoonishly reptilian eyes keen to every objection in my father's articulate defense. One time I was in the laundry room, sniffing fabric softener sheets, when I heard my dad arguing with Darren. "That's not behavior I think I can tolerate, can you?" he said. Then, "If you see things that way, you have some growing to do." Then, "Well, if that's how you think of me, there's little I can say or do to change your mind." It wasn't until I pressed my ear to the wall that I realized he'd been talking to Kermit. The next time I entered his office, I saw that my dad had moved Kermit's hands across his plastic eyes, covering them.

Sometimes, in pool season, Darren would let me start his car while he selected a cassette from the glove compartment. I'd pump the gas four times, counting, while Darren emptied the compartment to the floor, tapes, maps, a battery-less flashlight, and a Chinese take-out menu I'd been tearing into scraps and lighting with the car lighter whenever Darren left me in a parking lot. I liked the way you had to wait for the lighter to pop, the mystery of its ignition, the cigarette symbol etched into its top like a hieroglyph. I'd light a scrap, then drop it from the passenger window, the scrap curling in on itself, extinguished in a matter of seconds. Sometimes I'd pop the lighter again and stare at its glowing bull's-eye until it seemed like something I had never seen before. I liked doing things like that. Once, I remember Darren telling me he used to make himself cry when he was little by picturing the Earth seen from the moon, then farther away, then farther away, until the whole universe disappeared and all he could imagine was a huge widening white spot like a burn in a jammed film. I loved him for telling me that.

"You should have heard what the guy in front of me said to the bank teller," Darren said, returning with a Dum-Dum lollipop for me. It always disappointed me that Darren never said anything about me lighting the menu on fire. Sometimes I left it out on the passenger floor mat, hoping. "You would have loved it."

I unwrapped the lollipop, put my sneakers to the dash. "What happened?"

"The guy had his kid with him, and the kid kept reaching up to the counter, knocking things over, so the dad picked him up, but the kid started to cry." Darren gestured as if holding a kid. "So the bank teller said, 'Would a sticky make you feel better? Who wants a sticky? Who wants a super-special sticky?' and stuck a piece of mailing tape on the kid's hand." Darren stuck a piece of phantom tape to the dash. "And the kid looks at her, then back to his hand, and then just starts bawling. I mean *bawling*. And the father looks at the teller and says, 'Guess he don't like stickies.' "

"Guess he don't like stickies," I said, trying it out.

Darren clapped his hands together. "It's so *good*," he said.

Once, when we'd lived together, I found Darren sitting in the large bay window of our father's house, his legs drawn up underneath him, light slanting in through the blinds my father had resisted buying—he liked the way rooms looked starkly lit, an affection I've inherited, along with a habit of leaving my umbrella on subways—crunching an enormous red apple, the kind my father ate over the kitchen sink, rinsed, pared with a small knife. "Do you think dad minds me eating this apple?" Darren said, without looking at me. Outside, fat robins landed on the birdbath we'd always neglected to fill. I watched them hop into the grass as new ones, indistinguishable from the first, landed on the bath again.

"Do you think he'd be upset?" Darren said. He punctuated these questions with a sharp crunch of the apple. "He seems to like these apples so much." *Crunch.*

"I don't think he'd mind," I said. I pictured my dad the time I'd accidentally opened the bathroom door on him as he stepped from the shower, reaching for his robe. "Seems there's someone already in here," he'd said.

"But this is the last one." *Crunch.* "After this, it's strictly nada."

"It's not a big deal."

"But—it's a big apple," Darren said. *Crunch.*

"Dad doesn't care."

Darren took another bite, inspecting the mark his teeth had left. "Now that," he said, "is something I believe."

When we were little, Darren and I made a game of kissing our father on the lips. We'd wait until he thought we were asleep, then pucker like prom dates, making *coo-coo* noises. "Give us a keesh," we'd say, knowing he wouldn't, knowing he'd kiss the top of our heads like always. "We want a keeshy-keesh."

"There," he'd say, ignoring our request, pulling the sheets to our chins or turning off our night-light. It always depressed me when he turned off the night-light.

But the game was to turn your head at the last possible moment, so that his lips might find yours. "Sorry," he'd say, whenever this happened. "Didn't mean to get you."

"That was a keeshy-keesh."

"Yes, I guess so," he'd say.

"You gave me a keeshy-keesh."

"I guess I did," he'd say, standing, then leaving the bedroom door slightly ajar, the way we liked it. Years later, long after Darren and I had our own rooms, after Darren took to staying up late with his stereo on, just audible above the sound of my own breathing, I remember a dinner table fight that ended with Darren kissing our father on the head. "Keeshy-keesh," he'd said, standing behind him, lowering his lips to our father's hair.

"Stop it, Darren," our mother said.

"Mmm, but I like keeshy-keesh," Darren said, delivering another.

"Darren," our mother said, "that's enough."

"Never enough keeshes. Mmm, never."

I remember this: our father closed his eyes and placed his hands atop the table. I remember him doing that. "I don't know what it is," he said, "that is expected of me."

In pool season Darren dropped me off at my father's house. I'd gather my towel from the backseat, still damply chlorinated, malodorous, and discover that I couldn't think of anything to say, Darren with his hand on the gearshift, ready to leave. "Is that backboard still coming loose?" he said.

"Yeah. It falls down every time it storms."

"There's a bag of screws inside the pantry that would fix that," Darren said. "Inside a coffee tin on the bottom shelf."

"Thanks."

"That used to be a pretty good backboard," Darren said, waved, then pulled out of the driveway.

At night, in Darren's old room, I listened to the sound my electric fan made, the soothing whatever it kept trying to say. *You're going room-room.* Cars passed outside, sending elongated parallelograms of light across my walls, ceiling, and the sudden tombstone of my pool towel draped across a desk chair. I thought of Darren sleeping beneath the umbrella with his T-shirt across his face. I thought of the moment I said his name, the second that passed before he woke and lifted the shirt from his head.

Sometimes, when the car lights passed directly above my bed I could see the mural, a whale's eye, watching me.

Once, I saw one of the pool mothers' breasts. I was diving for Rex using a pair of goggles I'd found beneath the snack machine, kiddie-sized, with yellow lenses that made the world beneath the glimmering paisley top of the surface a sunken prairie, steeped in amber light. Legs moved awkwardly along this prairie, knees raised to support unsteady babies, feet moving as if to dance, readjusting, finding balance. Whenever new legs appeared, punctuated by a cloud of bubbles, they joined this dance, weight to one foot, then the other. I tossed Rex between dancers, catching him before he grinned his way to the bottom.

I saw a baby standing on his mother's knee. His mother held his hands, inviting him to dance, but his left arm slipped free and grabbed her swimsuit. When she pulled him away, his tiny hand flipped the top of her suit, exposing a small breast with a round, hard nipple. I watched it for a moment before the mother smoothed her suit back into place, the feeling of seeing something like that like the time I'd been reprimanded for not taking the trash out and, sulking my way along the path to the garage, moonlit, pebbled like a fishbowl, a falling star insisted I look skyward and made my errand, my resentment, and the breath suddenly suspended in my chest seem both negligible and holy.

Sometimes, when I saw Darren with his T-shirt across his face, or caught his reflection in the bay window, a thought came to me, sentence-like, italicized, inextinguishable. *I hate him*, it said. *I hate him*. "Darren," I'd say, wanting to erase it, needing him to look at me and make the erasure complete. "What are you up to?"

From the high dive you could see the grade school Darren and I had once attended before high school took him away, exchanging his windbreaker for a jean jacket, his sprint for a slouch. You could see the playground where Darren had once made me cry by telling me the plot of *The Day After*, which his class had been watching, inviting discussion, nightmares, while my class clutched an old parachute from the sides as our gym teacher threw kickballs on top, the balls momentarily vanishing in the chute's silky folds, then rocketing toward the sky when we pulled the chute back. We called this game "Popcorn."

"The first thing you'll do after they strike is cover your eyes," Darren said, "but it won't do you any good." He held his arms to his eyes, trembling with excitement. "Know why? It'll burn through your arms!"

"That's not true," I said, but the breath in my chest was suddenly incorrect, a trombone inside a pillowcase.

"Sure it is," Darren said. "And don't even think about jumping under a desk. You'll be a skeleton by the time you get there."

"It's not going to happen," I said, and my voice caught.

"Are you kidding? It's a miracle it hasn't happened already. It might be happening right now."

"Shut up!" I said, and burst into tears.

"Of course, we'd see a mushroom cloud."

The thing Mira was most afraid of was the Easter Bunny. "Not the cartoon one," she said. "Not the one in coloring books and stuff like that. The one at the mall. The one you're supposed to hug."

"I know what you mean," I said. We were squatting in the kiddie pool, watching the mothers take adult swim. It was the first time I'd been in a pool with a girl. "I was always afraid of looking into his mouth, seeing a face behind the mask."

Mira looked at me. "I was always afraid he'd know who I was," she said. "Like he might say, 'Mira, why didn't you return those library books? That's the same as stealing, you know.'"

I always liked it when Mira tried to make me laugh, but I felt guilty, too, since she was Darren's girlfriend, and he didn't know we sometimes talked this way. I thought about Darren teasing me in the car, his arm around Mira, the wind in his hair.

"Darren thinks you'll end up being a lot like your mom," Mira said.

"Really?"

"He says you're more like her," Mira said. "I think it kind of bothers him."

I tried to imagine Darren telling Mira I was more like our mother. The idea of a different Darren, confessing his worries, wondering about me, complicated my notion of the world. "But they're closer," I said.

Mira laughed. "Not really," she said. "Your mom's a hoot. Darren's more of a dark cloud." Mira adjusted her legs. "Like your dad."

I watched the mothers push themselves up out of the water. I watched them find their sunglasses and slip them on again.

"Darren's an unhappy camper," Mira said. "Sweet, but."

"A dark cloud," I said. It felt strange saying it.

"A dark cloud."

After a while, Mira said, "That's why girls will like you. You enjoy things."

"Darren enjoys things."

"Sort of. He likes making fun of things. Not exactly the same."

"He likes the funny things people say."

"If it proves they're dumber than him, sure."

"He likes you."

"Listen, Tim, I'm not saying I don't like your brother. I think he's great. He's very nice to me. It's just that—" she held up her hands, "I don't know. You see more things as you get older."

I saw the mothers lowering themselves back into the pool, towing their children in pink boats. I wanted to be with them, circling for Rex.

"I guess I shouldn't have said anything," Mira said. "Sorry, Tim." She described a semicircle with her hand. "Why don't you go see if you can drag him over here at least. Looks like adult swim is finished." She sat back against the edge of the pool. "Tell him he's needed," she said.

I stood from the pool and walked past the mothers, the kids, and the cracks in the cement slowly filling with water. My thoughts got mixed up in them somehow, the cracks. I followed them like they would lead me somewhere, but I couldn't tell if I was headed from the pool or from Darren. When I saw him, slouched into his chair, T-shirt across his face, my disorientation passed, and I remembered my message.

"Darren," I said. He lifted the shirt, regarding me like an intruder. His eyes squinted in the sunlight. "You're needed."

Sunday Wash

Jody found his mother's earring inside his sneaker. It was gold and spangly, a pearl at its center, edges flecked with tiny green stones that thrilled his palm. Jody set the earring on his dresser, then wrestled a T-shirt over his head. The sight of the earring beside his action figures raised a kind of question in him, but he couldn't tell what kind. From outside he could hear the ticking of the sprinklers Ron, his mother's boyfriend, had already turned on. Ron had been doing that ever since he'd moved in, running them in the morning, beating the sun to the punch. It seemed a strange thing to do, a prim but masculine gesture, like combing a mustache or chalking a pool cue. Once Jody had watched Ron as Ron knelt in the grass and drove a sprinkle into the ground. He'd tapped the spike into place with the heel of his hand, positioning it just so. When the spray angled across the property line, rainbows uncoiled themselves from inside, a surprise. Watching them, Jody felt a sudden longing for Ron, missed him like someone gone, which was confusing, since it was his father who was dead and Ron who wasn't.

The night before, Jody's mother had come into his room and sat on his bed, the sound of his electric fan marking the silence between them.

"Mom?" he'd asked, after a while.

"Yes."

"Did you want to say goodnight?"

"Yes."

"Okay, then." A pause. "Goodnight from me, too."

In the dark, Jody could not see her mouth, which troubled him; he wondered if she had whispered goodnight and he hadn't seen. It was horrible the way darkness worked.

"Don't forget about the hall light," he said. "Okay?"

A silence, which the fan neglected to fill.

"Mom?"

"Yessokay," she whispered. "The light." She stood from the bed, then closed the door behind her.

A moment later, the line of light beneath the door vanished. Jody searched the blackness where it should have been. The fan turned its eye upon him, blowing uncool air across his legs, side. Inside his stomach, things sparkled and crashed.

Once, Jody's parents had taken him to a holiday party—a grown-up party—where kids played in the basement while the parents danced above. Jody sat on the basement steps and watched three boys play a kind of Ping-Pong game where the loser had to stand against the washing machine while the others lobbed Ping-Pong balls at his crotch. When one of the shots ricocheted up the stairs, the tallest boy spotted Jody, and Jody was afraid they were going to make him play, too, but the boy only scooped the ball and asked, "You know that word 'duh'?"

Jody nodded.

"Well," the boy said, "I invented it."

Upstairs, Jody found his mother in the kitchen, talking with women who said "right, right, right" and held squat cups of wine like pet mice. He liked the way they laughed when his mother said funny things, enjoyed the feeling of passing through their laughter like a held door. He entered the living room; his father was not there. Men questioned him about Ping-Pong, school, Christmas. He used the bathroom, which had lit candles in it. He found his father in the guest bedroom, sitting on a bed piled with limp coats, petting a gray cat. Jody spotted him from the hallway, but waited, watching. His father had always been a quiet person, drawn to newspapers, long walks, and dim rooms. On Sundays, he preferred not to speak. Instead, he listened to Bach with a sofa cushion propped beneath his head, hands clasped atop his stomach, his fingers marking time, eyes closed. When the music finished, he put the cushion back into place, then brushed carpet lint from his legs.

"There's something wrong with this animal," he whispered, motioning Jody closer. He put his head to the cat's stomach. "Listen."

Jody listened.

"Do you hear that?" He rubbed the cat's ears, increasing the sound. "See?"

Jody watched him, and felt a kind of sorry he had never known before. "Dad," he said, "it's just purring."

His father looked at him. "Do you think so?"

"Yeah," Jody said. "Cats do that."

"Right," his father mumbled. "I mean, of course. Purring." He stopped rubbing, and the cat gave way to a silent yawn. "I guess I'm not what they call a 'cat person.' Although I don't especially like or dislike them. I guess I'm not what anyone would call an 'animal person,' am I?" He looked at Jody, and Jody wanted to bury his head in his arms.

"That's okay."

"Purring," he whispered, like it was an alien word, a medical condition, or nautical phrase.

"Yeah," Jody said, petting the cat again. "It's weird."

And this was the moment he'd turned over and over again, at

his father's funeral when he so badly wanted to cry—needed to cry—but couldn't. He thought of his father's hands down the cat's back, the movement of his fingers, his expression. There was a part of the conversation lurking just beneath this remembrance, a part that would allow him to grieve, but he could not find it again. It was when they'd stood from the bed, and the cat had jumped to the floor, scurrying away.

"You know," his father had said. "I was afraid he was dying."

Jody dressed and went downstairs. In the kitchen, dishes lay gleaming on the drying rack where Ron had stacked them, the sun catching on the rims of glasses and the legs of the thing you drained pasta in. All around, the countertops were piled high with his mother's papers: bills, receipts, letters, and catalogs that Ron had grouped into a kind of order, with catalogs all to one side of the sink, letters beside the microwave, and bills, receipts, and envelopes set out on the kitchen table, arranged by size. On top of each envelope, his mother's neat and furious script: "by September 3! get stamps! check for June statement—under car seat? glove compartment?"

During the week it was possible to avoid being alone with Ron, since Ron worked, but Sundays were a different matter. Saturdays, Jody watched cartoons on the little television in the guest bedroom until his mother woke, then followed her downstairs. He liked the guest room. It had a double bed that no one ever used and green, translucent curtains that made the room feel like the inside of a grape. It felt okay sitting on the edge of the bed with the television on and the light coming through. Sometimes Jody thought about what would happen if his mother and Ron came in and sat beside him, but that was a dumb thing to think about so he stopped thinking it.

Jody scooped some cereal straight from the box, then called his friend Tyler. It was too early to call, but he needed an escape, and the thought of hanging out in Tyler's basement, with its leather couches and satellite TV, where, at any moment, Tyler's sister Janeane might open the basement door and call down "did they want a grilled cheese?" was like hearing someone whisper his name across a dark room. He was rehearsing what he would say if Janeane answered when Janeane answered.

"Hello?"

"Um, is Tyler up yet?"

"I dunno. Hold on." A pause. A door sighing. Another pause in which Jody recalled the time he was walking his bike behind Janeane as she pushed her baby sister along the sidewalk in a stroller, the warble of the stroller's wheels enough to dissemble his own progress as they neared the neighborhood entranceway, where a green electric strongbox sat in the weeds beneath two pine trees. When they passed, Janeane pointed to it and said, "And *that's* where they keep the alligators," and Jody had felt something fine for her.

"He's still asleep," her voice said, now, blooming in his ear. "Who is this?"

Jody told her.

"Oh. Hmm. Well, I can wake him up. If you want."

"No, that's okay," Jody said. "Don't."

"He looked pretty asleep and everything. But I could."

"Naw. Let him sleep," Jody said, excited by the idea that they were deciding something together. "He'd get mad."

"Yeah."

He knew this was where he should say good-bye, but the sense that he was doing well prevented its passage.

"Hey," Janeane whispered, "do Mr. Ferguson."

"Eight-y five, star sticker. Nine-ty three, scr*atch* and sn*iff*."

"Nine-ty three, scr*atch* and sn*iff*," Janeane repeated. "Yeah. Okay. Bye."

By ten-thirty Jody's mother was still asleep. Jody went to the guest room and flipped through the TV channels, already knowing that he was going to turn it off anyway. It was terrible knowing things like that. Like the way he knew he was going downstairs to see what Ron was doing even when he put his ear to his mother's door and listened. Terrible.

Jody found Ron in the basement. He was sitting at his father's workbench, marking cardboard boxes with a thick black marker. He had his sleeves rolled up and a box tucked up underneath one arm, like it was a kitten he was trying to administer an eyedrop to. A round, saucer-shaped lamp hung above him, and the sight of its bulb burning again dipped into Jody's chest and ladled what breath was there.

"No chance you came down here to tell me how to spell 'miscellaneous'?" Ron asked. He did not look up.

Jody mumbled no.

"Well, that's okay," Ron said. " 'Stuff' sounds better anyway. Friendlier."

A few moments later Ron stood and wrestled the storm doors open. The way they folded back with a sudden creak and gasp had always frightened and exhilarated Jody on those few occasions he'd stood behind his father as he handed his bike up to him, the light hurting his eyes and the bike too heavy then nothing at all as his father freed it from his grasp. Now, Jody watched Ron lift a box and take it up the storm-door steps, balancing it on his shoulder. One of the things that Jody liked best about Ron was that he never tried to explain everything, the way most adults did. Another: he never said anything foolish.

Jody grabbed a small box, marked "Clothes," and followed Ron up the steps. He followed him across the lawn, his shoes making sucking sounds in the damp grass. At the end of the driveway, Ron's station wagon with its hatch open.

"Who knew you were my shadow?" Ron said.

After they'd finished loading everything, Ron closed the car's hatch, then studied his key ring. He glanced at Jody and Jody knew he was going to say something that was not "Would you like to come along?" but really was anyway. Jody looked away and thought of his mother, sleeping. He thought of her bedroom, closed and dark. He thought of her coming downstairs and seeing the papers arranged in little piles, and the idea of her sitting at the kitchen table informed him that he would say yes to the thing that was not "Would you like to come along?" even though saying yes confused him.

"Did you ever see so many keys?" Ron said.

———————————

Ron moved in at the start of summer. His first weekend he'd taken Jody and his mother to the movies, something they hadn't done since forever. Jody was excited to see his mother waiting in line under the lights just like everyone else, excited when the cashier handed her a ticket and she smiled and said thank you, simple as the string on a kite. Ron paid for everything and held the door for the two of them, glancing around the crowded lobby like it was an exam he'd neglected to study for. He wore a button-down shirt tucked into his jeans, his damp hair parted like a Cub Scout's. When he went to get them some popcorn, he returned with three jumbo buckets stacked on top of one other like a totem pole.

"Ron," Jody's mother said. "This is way too much popcorn."

Ron handed Jody the top bucket. "It is?"

"Yes, it is. It's—" she shook her head. "Ridiculous."

Ron sat next to her and placed a bucket on her lap. "You're right," he said. "This is way too much popcorn."

The lights went down. Jody turned his head aside so his mother wouldn't sense his laughter. He glimpsed Ron, his watch blinking in the dark, feet propped on the seat in front of him. Jody squinted, trying to read his expression. He saw the stems of his glasses, brilliant in the preview light. He heard music.

_____

They pulled out of the neighborhood and onto the small two-lane road that led to everything else. They passed things by. They passed the covered bridge where Jody's father had always slowed the car so he could see the stream moving underneath. They passed the kennel where you could sometimes see dogs following you along. They passed a couple on bicycles, the sight of their legs and knees reminding Jody that he, too, was moving through space, even though the car made it feel that this wasn't so. He saw Ron regard them in his side-view mirror and wondered if he was thinking the same thing.

They joined the highway. The sight of chain stores in the distance reminded Jody that he'd been glad the day of his father's funeral, when he'd ridden in the limousine with his relatives and had seen the stores with their lights on and cars pulling into the lots like always. He'd been happy about all the switches on the limousine door, too, which was wrong, and he'd liked the feeling of looking through tinted glass, which he shouldn't. At the reception afterward, he'd said the wrong thing to his aunt Gwen when she'd cornered him by the dessert table, lifting his chin from his plate of deviled eggs and shortbread cookies and asking, tearfully, what he thought about all this, and he had only thought to say, "Well, it's nice to see everyone again," and her eyes clouded with disapproval.

Ron turned off at the next exit. The ramp's curve was more severe than it looked and, from the back of the car, one of the boxes slid across the length of the interior and knocked into Jody's seat.

"Sorry about that," Ron said.

"It's okay," Jody said. He unfastened his seatbelt and turned. The box was tipped to one side, flaps open. One of his father's shirts lay tossed against the car door, folded. Its neat buttons and important collar accused Jody of a kind of injustice. Jody shoveled it back inside the box and quickly closed the flaps.

They stopped at an intersection. To the left, the Goodwill building. To the right, a new gas station with red-and-blue pennants stretched across its lot. A sign in front proclaimed "GRAND OPENING! 2 LTR COKE 1.09! DRIVE-THRU WASH!" But it wasn't the sign that drew Jody's attention; it was the bear. He stood in the grass beside the entrance holding a bouquet of balloons, waving one big paw at the stopped traffic. He had black fur and a frozen smile that looked more like a snarl. When the light changed, the bear turned his black gaze toward Jody, and Jody felt a terrible feeling.

"Hot day for that," Ron said.

"Yeah."

"The poor guy."

Two men helped them unload the boxes. One was older looking and heavy; he held a clipboard and checked things off while the other man, younger but with thick glasses, helped Ron carry some of the bigger boxes. Jody listened to the way the men spoke, trying to decide which one was more like Ron. He did this sometimes.

"Well, don't let Jerry chew your ear off over there," the clipboard man said. "Isn't that right, Jerry?"

"Okay," Jerry said. His voice was thick and wrong sounding. Jody watched as he heaved a box on top of a bin, his hair matted with sweat.

"You never know with Jerry."

There was still one item to be carried: the sheet-music cabinet Jody's father had planned to refinish but had never gotten around to. Jody had helped Ron carry it without the drawers, but now it lay heavy again, drawers in place, each brass handle as brilliant and solemn as a pigeon's eye. Jody followed Jerry's lead and got inside the car as Ron and the other man grabbed the top end of the cabinet and began to lift. For a moment the four of them raised the cabinet, together, and the feeling of that was like a barber's razor down Jody's neck. He struggled to keep his grip beneath the cabinet's base, until he felt Jerry's hand nudging his away.

"It's okay," Jerry said. "I goddit."

Jerry stood from the car, and Jody heard the cabinet drawers rattle and groan. The sight of the men lowering the cabinet to the ground made him look away. He sat where the cabinet had been and traced the carpet indentations in a desultory way, until he realized that the lines asked a serious question of him, and he hurriedly brushed them into nothing.

When they were about to leave, Jerry handed them a yellow receipt and a green leaflet. "This's for you," he said.

"That's a gift from Jerry, isn't it, Jerry?" the clipboard man said, then laughed. He was already opening boxes and tossing clothes into bins like they were loose apples.

Ron handed the leaflet to Jody. It was a coupon for a free car wash. On front, a drawing of the bear releasing balloons into the sky.

"Well," Ron said, "I guess we can't beat it."

"Yeah," Jody said, but at that moment the emptiness of the car closed in around him, and the sun breaking across the windshield reminded him that his mother would be up by now. She'd open the guest room door, expecting to find him in front of the little television. There'd be a space in the bedsheets from where he had been but no longer was.

The car wash was an abrupt cinder block structure with a clear plastic curtain hanging down across its front. The curtain was sliced into long strips. Steam rose from the spaces between the strips, as soapy water trailed out from underneath in a slow stream. Beyond the curtain, red spinning brushes swooped down from above, their ends spiking water. Whenever a car nosed through, the brushes descended upon the roof and made a sudden hissing noise.

Jody watched as the wash swallowed up another car. For a moment the car's taillights were bright inside the dark interior, until the curtain closed and the brushes swept down. Jody tried to follow them anyway, and was disappointed when the brushes rolled back to reveal an empty chamber with dripping water and a cloud of steam lingering like the punctuation of a magic trick.

"Looks like we're up," Ron said.

A slot in the floor track opened. Ron steered his front tires into it and put the car in neutral. The track made a loud clunking noise, then began to pull like an undertow. Jody looked up at the curtains as they knuckled across the windshield, expecting, for no good reason, to see people working them from above like marionettes. A sudden shot of water burst against the passenger window, immediately supplanted by the red-and-white whorls of a circular brush. Jody turned and gazed into its center, feeling as if the brushes were trying to call his name.

"Little noisy," Ron said, raising his voice above the drone of the machinery.

"Yeah," Jody said. He felt his face color because he knew Ron really meant "little scary" instead and was only trying to make him feel better. He kept his face to the window and balled his fingers into his palms.

It was darker now. A barrel-shaped brush descended upon the windshield. The barrel rolled to the top of the glass, then rolled back down, foaming, pressing. When it passed again, Jody heard a heavy clunking sound from underneath the car, followed by a second, quieter noise, and the car began to rock gently from side to side. They were stuck.

"Probably just slipped out of the track," Ron said, but Jody detected a false cheeriness in his voice that was unusual for him, and he felt alone. The brush swooped down again. Its cloth bristles flapped against the windshield in a kind of mockery, slapping the wipers and ridiculing Jody for hiding his head in his hands. Jody felt the car move again and felt the light through the spaces between his fingers and knew that they had passed through, but the wetness from his tears prevented him from removing his hands.

"Jody?"

His worst secret: sometimes when he dreamt of his father, it was Ron's voice that spoke instead.

"You okay?"

Jody turned to Ron and removed his hands. For a moment, he glimpsed Ron's face and saw that Ron was afraid of him, afraid of the tears and the breath heaving in his chest. He opened his mouth to release it all, but the only thing that surfaced was a horrible high squeak, like a parrot in a pet shop. He put his face to his hands and cried. All around them, red-and-blue pennants cracked in the breeze.

Jody had been wrong about his mother; she was not up. He stood at her door, listening, then gently turned the knob. Inside, the shades were still drawn, but it was light enough that he could see her. She had the covers pulled to one side, exposing one of her feet, while her hair lay neatly tucked behind her ear, as if she'd just fixed it. A squat glass of water sat on her nightstand, and Jody wondered if she'd gotten it while he was away, then crawled back into bed. The idea saddened him. He moved closer and considered sitting on her bed, but didn't. She had her hand on top of her pillow, and the sight of her wedding ring told Jody that he did not truly wish to wake her after all, as he had imagined. When he closed the door behind him, he thought he heard her move.

He went into the guest bedroom and turned the television on. The room was suffused in warm green light, but it did nothing for him. He sat on the bed and felt angry at himself for crying in front of Ron. How had he let that happen? It would be harder to be around him now, now that Ron had seen that part of him that was ugly and embarrassing. It was the part no one knew, the part that liked the limousine windows and luxuriated in the light beneath the bedroom door. It was the part that Aunt Gwen had glimpsed at the reception when he'd told her it was nice to see everyone again. The part that made her look away.

From outside, Jody heard kids' voices, shouts. He went to the window and parted the curtain, taking in a view of Tyler's yard, where a red football crested above the line of trees, then fell behind.

Jody took the stairs as fast as he could, jumping the last three. He opened the front door and escaped into the heat. Damp blades of cut grass stuck to his shoes, then fell away when he crossed the street. He ducked under Tyler's fence—how good it felt to put his hands to the ground, the surprising coolness there—and rolled into an envelope of trees. He stood and pushed through branches that tapped him on the shoulder and begged a moment of his time. And then, Tyler's yard.

"Jo-dee!" Tyler yelled. "Jody's here to save me!"

Jody shaded his eyes, and understood. They had Tyler by the legs and arms, Janeane and one of her lanky friends, carrying him like a heavy sack. Beside them, Tyler's baby sister, Megan, bonking Tyler on the head with the red football. Jody rushed toward them and grabbed Tyler by the arm.

"Theez boy cannot be saved," Janeane said.

"There eez no hope for theez boy," said the lanky friend.

"Yeah there is," Jody said.

"But, sir, you are mistaken," Janeane said. "Theez boy is doomed." She was wearing a white T-shirt and blue shorts, her hair clipped in back. When Jody grabbed her arm, he felt the delicate hairs there, and his throat burned. "They have a place where theez boy is going, a place they call—how you say?—de Spiderhole."

"Spiderhole," Tyler said. "No!"

"But yes, oh, yes," the lanky girl said.

They pulled him toward the slope of the side lawn where Megan was already leading the way. At the bottom, the backyard and patio, where two sliding glass doors divided the basement from the rest of summer.

Jody wrestled Janeane away, sending Tyler to the ground. Tyler grabbed Janeane's foot and she tumbled, taking Jody with her. Jody lay beside her, thrilled by her laughter and exhilarated by the closeness of their faces. Her look told him that he was safe with her, that she would never know the thing Ron now knew, that he could get away with being the person she thought he was forever. Forever. The idea of it roused a quiet laughter within him.

"What's wrong with theez boy?"

"Something eez wrong with eem."

Jody looked up and saw their faces looking down at him.

"There eez only one place for a boy like this."

"Yes, yes, eets true."

The two girls grabbed his arms, while Tyler, in a sudden change of loyalties, took his legs.

Jody cried for help.

"Oh, but there eez no help for a boy like you," Janeane said. Jody turned to her, but her face was masked by the sun. They passed under a tree, where Jody could see mottled light between the leaves. The leaves reminded him that summer would pass into fall and fall would pass into winter, the way they always did. Even a Monday became a Tuesday, and a week became a week later. Time would divide him from what Ron had seen today. There it was already, trailing in the grass behind them. How had he not realized this before?

It was cooler inside the basement, and dim. They carried him past the leather couches and the television set, then through the laundry area, where the clean smell of detergents was pleasing and heartbreaking. They entered a dark room.

It was the storage area, a part of the basement left unfinished. Jody could see pegboard along the walls, with rakes and shovels hanging down, and, looking up, pink fiberglass tucked into the spaces between the beams above. The light coming from the doorway caught in the fiberglass foil and in the piping from the hot water heater.

"Spiderhole," Tyler whispered.

"Spiderhole," the girls agreed.

At the base of the water heater, a little white pipe trailed out. The pipe ran along the wall, then curved into a hole between the water heater and the furnace. Whenever a tennis ball or racing car accidentally tumbled into its depths, whatever game it had been a part of immediately ceased. The hole was as wide as a garbage can.

"Beg," Janeane said, "and maybe we'll reconsider."

"Never."

"Pity, but don't they always say that?"

It was wet inside the hole. And cold. Jody's legs ached a little, and his arms hurt. In a moment, he would push himself out and wipe the dirt from his bottom, but for now he sat in the hole and watched their faces, regarding him. They were all so beautiful.

The Miles between Harriet Tubman and Harry Truman

If there's anything nicer than riding with the windows down, I don't know what it is. Especially when the driver is your long-lost father, as this one seems to me, and you've got your feet on the dash and the wind in your hair. Today my name is Nicholas, although my father does not believe me, I can tell. I introduced myself at the rest stop, but he only nodded and held the door, pretending he didn't understand. So that's where I get that from, I thought.

But isn't it windy, though?

In the rear-view mirror, I can see my brothers looking at me. Nate has his hand in his mouth, and poor Ricky is still snapping the ashtray back and forth; he's been doing that ever since I told him the news. I don't blame him, though. Ricky's sensitive, like me.

But isn't this the best car?

It's so plush inside, but solid, too—Dad wouldn't have it any other way. He's always had a penchant for economy and an eye for interior design. Remember the time we took those Christmas lights back, Dad? The ones that had the faulty blues—too dim—and didn't blink nearly as festively as the ones priced a dollar less, although the salesboy said otherwise. You know, I've always thought he was trying to prove something, Dad.

Don't flinch, Ricky! That's just me letting a little more air in.

Electric windows are just about the best thing, too. I especially like the noise they make when they slide out of view. I suppose there's a space down inside the door where it's all snug and soft, like the inside of an oboe case. You can explain it all later, Dad, if I ever think to ask.

We were waiting for Dad to fill the tank when I told them. Nate took the news in stride. He's older than Ricky, but younger than me. I think he was happy to find that he wasn't the oldest sibling after all. It must be a relief, finding out you're the middle child. The sudden license to underachieve. I look back and see him gazing out the window, his elbow resting outside, easing into the role.

"Well, I'll bet your mom will be glad to see you," Dad says. "She must be worried to death." Oh, Dad—so common!

"Oh, I don't know. She's always getting things mixed up."

Dad nods.

"Like last week she drove us to a Unitarian church. And we're Orthodox Catholic."

"Hmm."

"She didn't even notice until the third Joni Mitchell song."

"Is that right?"

"And by then it was too embarrassing to leave." I laugh. "But that's Mom for you."

Dad nods—I've caught him. He remembers. He reaches for the sun visor and pulls it down, trying, I suppose, to appear as if he doesn't. There are fishing flies hooked into the underside of the visor.

"I haven't gotten much better about the worms," I say. "In case you were wondering."

When Dad doesn't respond, I know he must be thinking about it.

"They still scare me a little. Squishy."

Nate leans forward and whispers something in Dad's left ear, the one away from me. Poor Nate. This was so long ago, when he was just a baby, a drooling blob inside his beechwood crib with me at the rungs, whispering good-bye.

"But I always remember what you said. How they were happy to be on the hook, how it was like being chosen. I think you always had a spiritual side that Mom never really understood. Did you ever feel that way, too?" I take one foot from the dash. "I've always wanted to ask."

I hear Nate whisper "Tell him stop," and hear Dad whisper something back, something like "It's okay"—I can't really tell, but I know how he would handle the situation, delicately, like spooning an egg into a pot of boiling water, which he did, every Sunday morning.

"I'm still trying to get the pancakes right," I say. "Mom says they're every bit as fluffy and light as yours were, but we both know she's just saying that. Do you remember what happened to that wooden spatula, by the way? I think the plastic one might be a handicap."

I notice now that although we're a quarter mile from the Harry S. Truman, Dad already has his blinker on. But that's like him, isn't it? Wanting to let everyone know well in advance. Aside from abandoning us with no explanation whatsoever, Dad has always been as respectful and courteous as a wine steward.

"No, I'm sure I don't," he says, and Nate gives him a look, then turns it on me.

"Tell him stop," he says. "Make him. *Please.*" And like that—bursts into tears.

Oh, Nate! I'd put my hand on your shoulder if I didn't think you'd pinch it.

"Yeah," Ricky says, then just keeps saying it. "Yeah, yeah."

Ricky!

Dad, always in control, tells them to quiet down, then, in the smooth, even voice that must have charmed Mom so many evenings ago, when he first placed his hand on hers and made that fateful proposition, says, "I'm not sure I know what this is all about, but I am sure that I don't like it." He looks ahead, of course, eyes always on the road. "If this is supposed to be a joke, it's not a funny one."

"Don't blame yourself, Dad," I say. "I shouldn't have pushed so much."

Dad doesn't say anything, though; he just slows the car into the Truman parking lot and, after mistakenly entering the truck lane, circles around back and stops the car in front again, where the grounds crew has already mowed the side islands of grass around the restaurant and has begun on the wider, longer stretches that extend past the tire shop. When I open the door I can see them in the distance, spewing grass into the air.

"Do you need anything?" Dad asks. "Money for a phone call?"

When I look at him I can sense his embarrassment in asking this. "Don't worry," I tell him. "It's not your fault." He makes a face that is a face wishing to understand, and I know that I'm doing the right thing, releasing him back into the quiet waters of his second life, the life he's built to forget the other.

"It's mine," I say. I wave to Nate and Ricky, but only Nate offers one in return. When the car pulls away I can see them in the rear window, my brothers, watching me get smaller and smaller until the car joins the interstate again, moving into the rush, and I disappear.

———

But that wasn't my father at all, was it?

How could it have been, when he's driving now, checking on me in the rear-view mirror? He's got the air conditioner on and, even from where I'm sitting, I can feel it upon my arms, cool, soothing. Dad would never have it any other way. All those open windows! Like I was a collie on the way to the pound.

In the passenger seat now, a black cello case, seat-belted in, as solemn as tombstone. Dad—a cellist!

"I play French horn," I say.

"Really? That's impressive. A very difficult instrument."

Well said, Dad. You always knew how to build, encourage, didn't you? Like the time I made a paper plane out of your doctoral certificate: you noted how the embossed seal acted as a kind of ballast to the heavy wings, giving the plane an equilibrium that loose-leaf paper could never achieve.

"I'm not very good. Mostly because something went wrong with my horn. I kept blowing and blowing into it and nothing came out. Nothing. We had to send it to New York to get it fixed." I shake my head. "You'll never guess what the problem was."

"A stuck valve?"

"A marble. There was a marble jammed into the tubing."

"Really? That's surprising."

"Mom acted like she was surprised, too, but I could tell she was just pretending." When I say this, Dad repositions his hands on the wheel, a gesture that pleases me. "I mean, it *is* pretty fun spinning marbles down a French horn—if you've ever tried it."

Don't shake your head, Dad! After all, you were the one who told me this story. How you spun a marble down your French horn just to see it go. Thinking it would come out the other side.

"Your mother did that?"

"I wouldn't put it past her," I say. Ahead, I see traffic merging left, passing the wide sweep of a mower, sending grass across the highway. When we pass, I see the face of the groundskeeper, and duck down out of view. "She can be like that sometimes."

Dad nods, and I hope I haven't upset him.

But doesn't he have the nicest glasses? Serious but light plastic frames that complement his brown-blond hair. Do you know I used to try your old wire-rimmed ones while you napped on the sofa? Dad, did you ever feel me releasing them, slowly, from behind your ears?

"She gets a lot of things mixed up."

"Oh."

"Like forgetting which rest stop—again." I click my tongue. "She's always getting the names confused."

"Truman and Tubman," Dad says, considering this. "It *is* a little confusing."

Oh, Dad, you always were so empathetic—in your own way, of course. Remember how you left us your snowblower for the winter months, an instruction sheet taped to the power switch?

"You don't have to worry," I say, and lean forward. "We're getting by." I consider putting my hand on his shoulder, but end up stroking the cello case instead. It's got a surface like a cantaloupe. "The important thing is not to blame yourself." I give a short, punctuating tap on the case. "That's what really counts."

Ahead, I see the Harriet Tubman at the top of the hill. There's one groundskeeper mowing around the flower bed that marks the entrance, and, as we pass, I see him mopping his face with his T-shirt, a kid with a ponytail. His legs are shagged with grass.

"I mean, Mom doesn't blame you."

Dad checks me in the mirror, then looks away. There's a second groundskeeper hacking the weeds at the base of the TRUCKS ONLY sign, shirt tied around his head, his chest bare and reddening in the sun.

"No one does."

When we reach the parking lot I point to the bank of pay phones just inside the entrance doors. "Well, there she is," I say. "Probably calling every rest stop within fifty miles." I offer a laugh. "You know how she can get."

But Dad doesn't say anything, though; he just waits as I open the door and feel the warm, grassy air rushing in. When I'm about to leave, he looks back and says, "Well, good luck" in a voice that could never be my father, and I feel this terrible feeling all inside my stomach. Like there's a bright bulb hanging there and the string suddenly pulled.

"Thanks," I say and close the door.

When he pulls away, I notice grass shavings blowing across the sidewalk, catching on pebbles, weeds, and the ends of my shoelaces.

But isn't the Tubman so much nicer than the Truman? For one thing, it's got a better view, higher up, where you can see cars coming in from miles away, and all the trees across the road, looking like they don't belong. Sometimes I wonder if they feel that way.

But the ice cream is the best thing. They've got this sundae bar with just about everything; all the Truman has is a soft-serve machine that hasn't worked right since the time I poured M&Ms in the top.

When I get to the bar I see Henry eyeing me from the back register. He's got some new girl working the toppings, too pretty to work here long, and, when she asks me what I want, Henry walks over and starts scooping me a bowl of marble fudge, my usual.

"You supposed to be over here today?"

"I dunno," I say.

"You dunno, huh?" He ladles in a topping of Heath bars on one side, M&Ms on the other. "How come you dunno?"

I shrug.

Henry hands me the bowl. "That's a whole lotta 'dunno-ing.'"

But aren't the booths here the most comfortable ever? They've got a few tears in the vinyl, here and there, but what can you do? It's way better than the Truman, with all those hard plastic swivel chairs that make you feel like you're ten feet from the table. If I ever get a house, I'm going to get a booth just like the ones they have at the Tubman. I'll put it right in my kitchen. I'll eat cereal there.

When I finish my sundae, I notice that Henry isn't standing behind the bar anymore, just the girl, who is reading a magazine across the fixings, which Henry would never allow.

And I get a feeling.

I throw my bowl into the trash and head out to the parking lot, where the groundskeepers are now mowing the grass around the wheelchair ramp. Shavings litter the walkway and, after the mowers move on, I stand at the top of the ramp and kick as much grass as I can off the side, walking down, then starting at the top again to touch up the spots I missed. I like the feeling of that, of making it nice and clear. This little scene plays in my head where someone is thanking me for it, over and over again, like it's the biggest deal in the world.

"That's okay," I whisper. "It's nothing."

———

But how strange to meet your new wife, Dad. Especially on a day like this, with the sun just beginning to set, and all the day's heat rising from the road. I liked the way she insisted on sitting in the back, saying she wouldn't dream of making me sit back there with the baby, but, in the end, relented anyway. I think I like her, Dad.

But what's with this baby?

He's the sleepiest baby I've ever seen. He didn't even move when I touched his tiny hand and stroked his tiny fingers. Not even a tiny blink. Did I used to be the same way?

"I just feel so bad for your mom," Dad's wife says. "She must feel so bad. But I could see myself making the same exact mistake. I really could."

"Well, I'll tell her you said that," I say, and note Dad's expression.

"Oh, please do."

"This isn't the first time this sort of thing has happened, though."

"Oh?"

"Last week she was supposed to pick me up at my friend Jim's house, but she ended up at my friend John's house instead, and John isn't even really supposed to be my friend anymore, ever since he told all these lies about me, but there Mom was, knocking on his door."

"So what happened?"

I really like her, Dad—she's terrific, the way she turns and meets your eye. Those kinds of things mean the world, don't they?

"She ended up talking with John's mom for a while, until they figured out the mistake, and then my mom called over to Jim's house and they all laughed about what a funny thing it was, mixing them up like that."

She laughs, a good, solid laugh, and for a moment it's like I'm a little in love. "The poor woman," she says.

But doesn't the baby make the funniest sound when he yawns? Like a cap twisting, that sudden *psst* of air.

Dad, you do not laugh. You look ahead, not wanting to be part of this conversation. Why? Are you remembering the time you told me to look for deer in the painting above the television? How you told me they emerged every time I looked away, prancing behind trees and poking their heads through the shrubbery in the foreground. How I stayed up until midnight with binoculars around my neck, a blanket to my chin. You know, I've always thought that experience helped me develop a sharper eye for detail. If we get the chance, I'll show you some of my watercolors.

"I won a ribbon," I say. "For a painting I did."

"That's great," Dad's wife says, as Dad nods and says the same.

"It was a painting of our old house. The one with the tree fort." When I say this, Dad looks away, like he's checking the side-view mirror, and clears his throat.

"It was hard, getting it right. I couldn't remember whether the ladder had four steps or five."

Don't make that face, Dad, please! The memory of the night I "ran away" from home is one of the sweetest ones I have of you, you bringing me an extra pillow and blanket, and that bag of potato chips we shared under the tree-fort roof, as rain began to beat against it. I remember telling you I was sorry for running away, but it just had to be, the way you nodded and said you understood, leaving me a flashlight as you descended the ladder and returned to the house, watching me, I could tell, from your bedroom window. The shock—and pleasure—of waking up in my own bed the next morning, the sun coming in, the flashlight tucked just underneath the pillow.

"I'll never forget," I whisper.

"Oh, things like that you never do," Dad's wife says.

Before we pull in to the Truman, I take my library card from my pocket and slide it under the baby's car seat. He doesn't move when I do this, just does the same baby-nothing he's been doing the whole time. I watch him for a moment, then I push the card underneath a little more, out of view. Dad, when you find it, please tuck it inside that black imitation leather wallet I gave you so many Christmases ago, the one you said was so much roomier than your silver billfold. I like the idea of you having it with you.

Outside, I see stiff weeds around the welcome signs, like shadows underneath: the spots the groundskeepers missed.

"You can just drop me off at the entrance," I say.

"Oh, of course not," Dad's wife says. "We don't mind." She turns to give me a smile and puts a hand on my knee. "Besides, I'm sure your mom would like to meet us. Just to put her mind at ease."

"Well, that's the thing," I say. "She gets kind of scared meeting new people. I mean, not that you're scary or anything, it's just that—" I look at her, wanting to let her know, when, out of nowhere, the baby starts to cry. Big, end-of-the-world crying, so loud that my eyes begin to tear.

Who knew he had it in him?

When I open the door, Dad's wife steps out and gives me a hug, right there in the parking lot, right in front of everyone, then takes the baby from the car seat and holds him for a while.

"I'll tell her how you wanted to meet her," I say.

"Please do."

She bounces the baby, gently, calming him.

Dad, she's wonderful. I understand why you do not rise now and put your arms around me, too. I understand why you take a pacifier from the glove compartment and wipe it clean. I see you doing that, Dad. I see you watching them, your wife and child, and I understand. As only a son could.

Before they pull away, I feel a hand upon my shoulder, and I know.

"You're really in for it this time, Buzz," a voice says, but I just keep waving. Dad's wife waves back, holding the baby's arm in hers, puppeteering. "I've never seen her so mad before."

I nod, watching the baby's arm, a pale comma against the window, diminishing.

But wasn't that Dad honking the horn good-bye?

The garage behind the Truman has always reminded me of an airport hangar, with huge, windowless doors that close with a roll of thunder and a high, ribbed roof that makes a noise like applause when it rains. Sometimes I throw a tennis ball against the doors when no one is watching, when all the mowers have left and the only groundskeeper is Sam, who never seems to mind. Stacks of tires rise to the tops of the doors, the biggest at the bottom, then getting smaller and smaller, like a totem pole. Air filters sag from brackets on the wall.

"She's in the break room," Sam says, leading me past a row of white pick-up trucks with DIVISION OF HIGHWAYS on the side, and mowers roped into the beds. When we get to the door, I hear her talking to Pauline inside.

Sam puts a hand on my shoulder and whispers, "Good luck."

"Thanks," I say.

When I enter the room I see my mom sitting with Pauline at the table closest to the snack machine, the one with my initials carved underneath. Pauline has her feet on a chair, shirt sleeves rolled up, exposing her too-red arms, and Mom has her hair in a bandanna, a U of sweat showing through her T-shirt. The bottoms of Pauline's boots are as green as limes.

"Don't worry," Pauline says, spotting me first, "you don't have to kiss us."

Mom doesn't laugh. I look away.

"Well, I'll see you next week, Karen," Pauline says, leaving me her seat. When I take it, Mom lights a cigarette and drags a foil ashtray closer to her.

"Mom, I'm so . . . sorry," I say, and all this weird feeling finds a passage in my stomach, and passes through.

"Don't," Mom says, holding up her hand. "Even."

We sit that way for a while, not saying anything. Sometimes I look over, hoping she'll meet my gaze, but she only looks toward the door, as if I were still standing there. There's grass in her hair, and I want to brush it away.

"I looked for you, when I was out there. Working. I looked at the faces of drivers and the faces of people in the passenger seat, thinking the next one might be you. I looked at all those cars passing by."

"Mom, I'm—"

"But they never were you. Always someone else. Some other family with some other kid, going some other place."

The feeling finds a second passage, a corridor to the base of my throat. "Mom," I whisper.

"All those people, going all those places." She shakes her head. "I've never really looked at them before. Not like that, anyway. Isn't that strange?"

"Mom . . . I'm so sorry."

"I know I'm some kind of disappointment to you, Buzz. You want some other kind of mother."

Before I hear myself tell her no, I feel tears on the back of my hand, which has arrived at the bridge of my nose. "I don't want some other kind of anything," I say.

"Most days I wish I was that other person, Buzz. I really do. But I can never be. That's what I was thinking today, watching all those cars. It was the loneliest feeling."

I put my hand to her arm. "Please."

"I don't know anymore, honey. I know that I've tried. And I know that you're a good kid. You really are. But it's like I know how much better things could be, and the knowing is killing me. It is."

I bury my head into her arms. She strokes my head for a while, and the whole time there's this crazy sound coming from my chest, like an owl's call, *ooouh-ooouh*, but I can't make it stop, and then Mom is crying, too, and it's like I don't even know what's happening anymore.

"I called grandma and grandpop while you were away," she says. "I'm so sorry, honey."

And it's like the owl sound finds its way into my mouth. *Noouh-noouh.*

"It'll just be for a couple of months. Just until I can . . . straighten some things out. It'll be better for you. Better there."

"No," I say, "please, Mom, don't. I'll never, again. Never."

"It's nothing you did, honey. It's just about . . . better."

"But I can be. Better."

"Maybe we both can. Someday."

I don't know how we leave the room. I don't know how Mom opens the truck door, and I don't know how I end up in the truck bed, with a big mower staring me down, all ropes and crusted grass, and I don't know how a blanket got back there, coarse and woolen, but there I am, sitting on it, as we pull out of the garage and head out onto the interstate. I'm looking down so long I don't even notice the grass at my feet, and the grass underneath the blanket, and the grass blowing out of the cab, trailing behind us under the pink-green sky.

What brings me back are the crickets. There are crickets hopping out from underneath the mower, and crickets lighting on the sides of the bed, gray ones and black ones taking flight, chasing the grass. One lands on my arm and one lands on my shoulder, bucking the breeze. After a while, one takes off, but the one on my shoulder stays, watching me. I like him. I like the way he moves his legs together and I like the way his little antennae bend in funny ways.

So I cup him in my hands. He makes this crazy pulsing between my palms, tickling, but then I feel him calming down, a slower, relaxed pulse. I think about what I'll do with him when I get him home. How I'll put him in a jelly jar with holes punched in the lid. How I'll put him by my nightstand and say goodnight to him when grandma leaves the room. How I'll see him in the morning, resting in the grass. And then I close my palms together until the pulsing stops.

The
Houses
Left
Behind

---

18 Sampson Street

The first house.

For Donna, bright windows, spun mobiles, and limp towels along her underside. For Teresa, her older sister, the rumbling of crib bars between her fingers. Donna's surprise at this: noise from silent things. Teresa's disappointment in Donna, the dull fact of her, like a broken shoelace. They've moved the crib into the parents' bedroom, as they did when Teresa was Donna's age.

Do you know that you've sucked my finger for an entire car ride? Teresa wants to say.

Kitchen, 18 Sampson

Refrigerator: avocado green. Makes an interesting space when Dad opens the door. Sometimes Teresa remembers that space—the way light flooded in from above and below—but cannot place it. Sometimes this happens in restaurants or malls.

Teresa remembers:

Donna in her high chair, crying. Their father with a spoonful of yellow goo, twirling it in time to a little song. The high chair made a squeaking noise when you pressed the armrests. Although it was once fun to sit in the chair—the view!—it no longer was. The tray was irritating, confining. Sometimes Teresa eats entire meals standing beside her kitchen sink, wandering into the living room to change the radio stations with a paper napkin in one hand and a spoonful of couscous in the other.

Donna remembers:

Cold floor! Cold, cold, cold. Pull with hands, legs will follow. Grate beneath refrigerator can be removed, but yields little behind. Shadows underneath table much more fun. If cat is on chair, let him be.

Nowadays Donna keeps her house immaculate. Friends say.

Fruit bowl, blue, from interim town house, address forgotten

Soft grapes for Donna. Dad likes bananas lopped into cold cereal and sour green apples, split in two and dunked in peanut butter, which Mom says is a waste. Teresa likes pears because no one else does. Pears are her thing. Hers.

The town house is temporary, the parents say, so make do. "Make do" means boxes in every room and no curtains in the dining room. Teresa's first meal in a room with no curtains, a revelation, the pleasure of stark trees outside and the clinking of glasses inside, while cars pass in and out of the neighborhood drive, unaware. Sometimes, all at once.

But the windows are so dirty. Later, their mother cleans them with a striped rag, squirting cleaner from a bottle. The house brightens. One morning Teresa finds the glass cleaner next to the fruit bowl and squirts a little onto the grapes, but then feels guilty and rinses them over and over again, apologizing to the sink, hand towel.

That night Donna is sick. Teresa can hear her in the bathroom. So she goes to her bedroom and closes the door, but the room accuses her anyway. The room she and Donna share, twin beds divided by a single nightstand. On Donna's side, a library book, mysteriously titled *Your Skin Holds You In!*, on Teresa's, a book about jewelry she got two birthdays ago. Whenever Donna is out of the room, Teresa steals a look at the *Skin* book. It has pictures of kids bobbing for apples and swimming in brown rivers, diving from tall rocks. "Let's go!" the text reads. "Again!" It bothers Teresa that Donna has never asked her what the title means. Bothers her that she wouldn't know either.

When Donna returns, Teresa feigns sleep. But she can't stop her legs from shaking. She has a notion to crawl into bed with Donna and have Donna tell her made-up stories until the world spins back into order, but she discovers she can cry without making any noise at all, and the notion passes.

Concealment, third house

The closet inside the laundry room, where their mother keeps detergents, fabric softener, and, after Thanksgiving, stocking stuffers hidden inside an empty Amway box. The girls find them every year, but manage to fake surprise anyway. That their parents never catch on saddens them both, although they never discuss this.

The attic with its stringed door, like a lost balloon.

"We should get the exercise bike out of the attic," their mother says, absently, after dinner.

"I thought we got rid of that," their father says.

"No, it's still up there. Somewhere." She looks up to the ceiling, even though this is ridiculous (another floor separates them), but the idea of the exercise bike hidden above their heads thrills Teresa, and she shoots a daring look toward Donna, whom Teresa knows is afraid of the attic, since she screams every time Teresa jumps for the string, missing it by feet.

Framed posters

Mean the move is real. The commitment of nails, brads. A poster hangs in each of the Addison Circle bathrooms, of which there are four, the roomiest house yet. There are two sinks in the master bath, and a little red ceiling lamp that makes the room glow like the inside of a toaster.

---

101 Addison Circle

For Donna, the first bedroom that is all hers. The trip to the carpet outlet with her mother, picking one out. The feeling of walking across each, the salesman saying things to them about wear, durability. When Teresa knocks on her door now, it is like a visit, and Donna's heart goes weird inside her, but she tells Teresa to leave her alone. She spends hours observing herself in the mirror. Is this really how she looks?

For Teresa, her first notion of property. Property as a thing you can have. The trees, the fence, the newspaper on the walkway, theirs. The fence separates their property from their neighbor's property, and this is nice for everyone. It does not mean that they do not love their neighbor, as they have been instructed, nor does their neighbor not love them. The neighbors have holiday parties. The neighbors wave when waved to, and rake their leaves in the fall. The neighbors have other homes with other kids. When Teresa thinks of those kids now, she sees their properties as distinctly as their faces, recalls the places where the lawn dipped, threatening ankles, or which rooms were forbidden to enter (like the Jamisons' dining room, with an antique doll encased in plastic at the center of the table—creepy, even now), all the indelible associations: Paul Oglesby, a swept garage with no cars inside; Gretta Anderson, a pink bedroom with water stains on the ceiling; and Susie Green, forever the slatted shadows beneath a screened-in porch.

Sometimes, when Teresa visits Donna's home, she brings bags of fast food for the kids, partly because she wants to be the cool aunt, bringer of fries, shakes, but mostly because she loves the moment when Donna makes them wait until all the bags have been emptied and divvied out onto heavy dinner plates, the momentary silence it brings, the narrow kitchen a sudden cathedral.

Ideas of abundance, Addison

Wrestling a seventh bar of Dial from the package beneath the bathroom sink.

The time the trashmen wouldn't haul away the last two bags of autumn leaves. Burning them instead.

Needing a paper towel and tearing off three.

The way heat caught in the space above the staircase, surprising you.

Leaving the cat in the basement with a food dispenser, water bowl, and litter box. His reluctance to return.

After storms, the driveway riddled with worms.

Teresa babysits Donna, and makes a discovery

She enters Donna's room, and sees her sleeping with the bedsheets balled into her hands, mouth open, hair shot up like a pineapple's stalk. Teresa knows there is a feeling she is supposed to have, standing in the doorway, watching her sister, but it fails to find her. In its place, another: I don't really love her. She lets the notion ride. It feels misplaced and thrilling. Donna is, after all, an embarrassing sister. It's dumb, having to feel that she loves her in spite of everything she usually feels for her. Having to feel guilty for thinking otherwise. Having to put an arm around her in holiday pictures and screw up her mouth in ways it rarely goes. Having to say good morning, goodnight.

Earlier, she'd heard Donna climb into the family room sofa bed, the creak and sigh of its joints as Donna slipped inside and, despite all physics, pulled the mattress back into place. Teresa jumped on top, wanting to hurt her just a little, but Donna only laughed and shifted so that Teresa no longer felt the bulge of her beneath the cushions. How had she done so?

"Get the hell out of the sofa," Teresa said, forgetting to disguise her amazement. Then, "You're so stupid."

"Stupid. Oh, stupid," Donna sang.

"That's right. That's what you are."

"Dat's me. Oh me, oh my."

Teresa punched the cushions.

"Careful," Donna warned, "the cushions are electricity."

Teresa stood and yanked the bed frame out, sending Donna's pale, nightgowned body to the floor. She curled into a ball, laughing without making noise. Lint stuck to the backside of her legs.

"Stop. Being. Stupid," Teresa said, thinking, *She's smarter than me. It's true.* She grabbed Donna by the wrist. They wrestled. For a moment, Donna had Teresa pinned, her face flushed with color, surprise, until Teresa felt her release her hold and allow her the advantage. The gesture confused the older sister, and made the world seem less kind.

"Don't do that," she said.

"Don't," Donna repeated.

Teresa straddled her chest. "Do you understand?"

Donna laughed. Teresa pulled her knees in closer, digging into her sides.

"Do you?"

Donna looked up at her as if she were a pinwheel blowing in the breeze.

"Don't ever."

Sale

Donna's junior year, her parents put the Addison house up for sale. A "white hot" market, the Realtor says, and her parents carry this phrase around like a closed umbrella, releasing it at dinner, over the phone, and inside car interiors, giving Donna an uneasy, unlucky feeling. The Realtor's name is Fran, a small, nervous woman whose pantsuits always have cat hairs on the sleeves and whose emphatic, unsure sentences make her seem a kind of understudy for another, more confident Realtor who never arrives.

"Are these the original moldings, or?" she says, appraising the dining room doorway.

"No," Donna's mother says, explains.

"Right, right." Then, "So do you usually keep these shades drawn, or?"

"Oh, I just closed those the minute you pulled up. Should I open them?"

"No, closed is fine. Nothing wrong with closed. Unless."

In this manner they tour the house. Donna follows. She feels a kind of kinship with Fran, since Fran is awkward in a way that she privately feels herself to be, and she's excited by the possibility of watching her mother tolerate behavior from another that she would criticize from her. Later, she will explain this to Teresa.

"I could tell Mom wanted her to shut up, but she couldn't say anything. Like we went into your old room and the Realtor said we should angle your bed diagonally from the wall and—you'll love this—take down 'that funny horse picture.'"

Teresa laughs. "What did Mom say?"

"You know, something like 'that's certainly an idea.' I don't even remember now."

"Did she take it down?"

"No, but we did angle the bed. All three of us. It was weird. Like we were moving a set around." Donna pauses. "It felt funny to have a stranger in your room. Even Mom being there was kind of weird. We were all just standing there in the space where the bed used to be, not saying anything. After a while, we sat on the bed together."

"I used to dream of things like that," Teresa says.

Teresa, away at college, sharing a house with three roommates. Donna has visited only once, for a long weekend, sleeping on a futon mattress and sitting cross-legged at a secondhand coffee table, her first taste of sushi, saki. She had been surprised by the roommates, the way they slunk around the house, mumbling inside jokes and criticizing the fourth roommate, away at home. Donna listened, trying to decide which one of them she was most likely to become, a grim sentencing she'd taken to lately. She watched the way Teresa reacted, her gestures, wisecracks, and felt that she no longer knew her. She listened to Teresa, as Teresa stood to pantomime something the fourth roommate had done recently, and longed for the attic door again, with Teresa jumping for the string.

"It's horrible, isn't it?" Teresa said.

"What is?"

"That someone would do that," Teresa said.

A month before Christmas, Donna finds the Realtor's For Sale sign in the garage. Upside down against the garbage cans. When Donna asks her parents about it, they tell her that they've decided against moving for now, and a little silence spreads through the room, like a crack in a windshield. Later, Donna helps carry Christmas ornaments out of the basement. Mixed in with the nativity set, tree stand, and coils of outdoor lights, a box of books Teresa has left behind. Donna opens the box and glances at the covers, then pushes the box to "Teresa's side" of the basement, a distinction that has never struck her as odd.

In winter

The heater makes noises like dropped pennies. Donna sleeps with her socks on. In every window, an electric candle that flickers like the real.

Kinds of doors

Sliding. Donna's first apartment. These divide her from a parking lot and a twenty-four-hour gas station, where she sometimes sees a homeless man screaming into a pay phone, one hand to his free ear, fending off noise. The sight of him gives Donna a kind of optimism, although she cannot explain what kind. On weekends her boyfriend, Paul, visits, and they walk around the city, eating meals they are not hungry for, and nearly buying things they relinquish at the last moment: remaindered books, antique picture frames, cool shoes. One time, Paul says, "If I lived here, I would never stay inside," and Donna feels a sharp pinch she does not wish to recognize. When Paul leaves, she lowers the security bar to the sliding door, and calls Teresa for the first time in months.

Pocket. Between the kitchen and living room. Rarely closed, except when Teresa gets take-out Vietnamese and a video. She likes doing that, especially on a Friday night, when it's nearly dark and the sense that she should be out, doing things, *meeting people*, shows up like a weed.

The door slides heavily along its track; Teresa must use both hands to slide it all the way. There's a brass lock that can be locked, if she wishes, but why? What *does* she wish? She wishes she had gotten an extra order of spring rolls. No, that's not it, she thinks, but then the video begins, and she must chide the previews and snap her chopsticks in two. She sips beer from a frosted glass.

Screen. Teresa and Donna sit in Donna's new kitchen, which still exudes the smell of paint, despite the breeze moving through. Outside, Donna's children, Matthew and Jason, take turns jumping into an inflatable pool that Teresa thinks looks too flimsy for that sort of thing, but what does she know?

"We've got roofers coming in tomorrow, and electricians on Wednesday," Donna says, scribbling this onto a Post-it note. "You can just leave the garage door open all week, if you want. Makes it easy."

But the idea makes Teresa just the opposite. House-sitting is, for her, an intimate, but practical proposition, like getting a haircut. She feels both pleasure and embarrassment in stripping her sister's bed (her sister and husband's bed) and wadding up the children's pajamas from the closet hamper, separating dark and light. At night, Teresa hears dogs barking. She lies awake, listening. Their barks seem a kind of argument where both sides have long since agreed, but have failed to notice. She understands this for only a moment before sleep, until the following night, when the idea shows up again, renewed.

A collapse of houses

The year Donna's marriage falls apart, her parents buy a house at the beach. Come, they say. Bring the kids.

So she brings the kids.

For Matthew, his first shower out of doors, standing inside a wooden stall where his grandparents have left their bright flip-flops and limp bathing suits, like honeymooners. He is not sure whether it is right to remove his suit or not. (Is an outdoor shower still a shower?) He begins to untie the knot, and is pleased when the straps resist, too wet to pull apart. The water stings his legs at first, but Matthew lifts them anyway, allowing sand to pass from the bottom of his feet and the spaces between his toes. The house is supported by wooden posts, wide as garbage cans, cracked in places. At night, Matthew thinks he feels the house rocking in the breeze.

Jason, younger than Matthew, complains whenever his mother makes him come home from the beach. The beach is where his bucket is. He builds sand castles near the ocean's edge, in the flat apron of sand that makes sucking sounds when he presses the bucket into it. He must reshape the top of the pressings himself — it bothers him that he cannot make them perfectly flat again — or they crumble and crack. He puts shells inside the castle walls, since they enjoy this. Once, a hermit crab emerges, testing the walls. Mom, Jason says. Look.

But his mother is asleep beneath a striped umbrella, a towel covering her eyes.

If I remove the towel, Jason thinks, but doesn't.

When he looks back inside the castle, the walls have slumped and the hermit crab is gone. Jason takes his bucket and begins again, thinking, *This time better, more, more.*

Nights, the guest bed sags, so Jason sleeps on the floor, the bedspread folded beneath him, the top sheet a lean-to roof, stretched from the bed to the ground. Mornings, the roof around his ankles.

Where books are mentioned

Matthew reads C. S. Lewis and J. R. R. Tolkien, although *The Lord of the Rings* confuses him at times. His bookmark tarries in the early chapters of *The Two Towers*, as if exhausted by the proposition of the pages that follow. So many dense forests to trod. So many orcs. His father gave him *The Return of the King* for his birthday, and Matthew has taken this along with him to the beach, where he sometimes reads the first few pages before falling asleep. Other times, he fans the pages before his nose, the thrill of a new book, the inner sweetness of its gluey spine.

Jason re-reads Hardy Boys books, although he has been assigned *A Day No Pigs Would Die* (everyone says it is sad) and *Where the Red Fern Grows* (the class saw the movie the year before, also sad). Jason is weary of sad. So he revisits *The Secret of the Old Mill*, his favorite, after *The Shattered Helmet*, which has better illustrations and isn't nearly as heavy on Chet. But, lately, the *Mill* has been speaking to him. He likes the idea of the abandoned mill, mysteriously lit at night, while Frank and Joe prowl the grounds, looking for ways to peer inside. It is dark out, but so bright inside the mill. Light slants from inside, drawing the boys closer. In a moment, they will ride the waterwheel to an open window, hanging from the ledge. The idea of them looking inside grasps something Jason cannot explain. He wants to take whatever it is with him. He wants to roll it up inside his jeans and carry it around for awhile.

He reads until his eyes make tiny clicking sounds, then turns off the light.

The houses left behind

Teresa's sometime meditation, when her own house is too quiet, and she cannot sleep.

So go through a room, she thinks, although it does not feel like a thought. It feels like snapping a towel, or tucking the spout on a carton a milk. *There!*

In the Addison house, start at the bedroom door—closed—and open it. Does it open in or out? In. It is an unusually light door, unpainted, unfinished. It smells like pine (too ordinary). What else? The knob makes a clunking noise when turned all the way to the left. Better. The knob has a hole in the center, purposeless, wide as pen refill. Closer. You can look through the hole and see light sometimes. Open. The bed is never made.

Remember Richard's parents' house (a college boyfriend), the feeling of skylights and ceiling fans, like a ski lodge. Richard's moodiness all tied up in it, in the squares of light across the family room floor, the clicking of the ceiling fan chain marking the times he left the bed without explanation, stealing into the smaller guest room where no one ever slept. Thinking: *A marriage like that.*

Now Donna's room. Addison. The summer between your first and second year of college, when the mystery of the interior spaces imploded, suddenly, like underbaked bread. Your room felt hot and cramped, especially with the sewing machine Mom installed in your absence, patterns laid out across the space where your beanbag cushion used to be. Your walls, posterless and painted over, had the neat and cheerless aspect of a waiting room.

But Donna's room was the same: lavender walls and a cream-colored bedspread, a floor lamp pulled to the bedside, with fashion magazines tented over its base. You found her reading one with the radio on, wearing shorts over her bathing suit, her hair still wet from an early swim. In the moment before she heard you in the doorway, you saw Donna as she truly was: relaxed, comfortable, eased into an early maturity that had always eluded you, her pink tummy lipped over the edge of her shorts. Despite everything, she'd become someone you wanted to be.

"You shouldn't go out in the sun like that," you said.

"I'm in."

"You're red as an apple."

Donna flipped a page. "More like an eraser."

From the radio, a syncopated beat like a flat tire. Between it, a woman singing about men who got away.

"You know," you said, "that stuff can turn to cancer. Maybe not now, but later. Like in twenty years."

"Twenty years," Donna said. "Something to think about." She crossed her legs in an unflattering way. But how had she gained the advantage in doing so?

"You know," you said, "you really are getting fat, Donna."

She put the magazine down. Her eyes were slick and gorgeous.

"Don't worry," she said. "One day you won't even recognize me."

Burial

Their father dies in August.

Teresa and Donna help their mother put the beach house up for sale. They put things in boxes and drive them to the storage facility lot, where the long rows of squat garages seem another unnecessary reminder of death. Inside, their father has left everything stacked in meticulous order: furniture wrapped in soft cloth, auto parts—why did he save auto parts?—in blue Rubbermaid tubs, and boxes of clothes, books, and whatever else stacked on top of wooden palettes, eluding whatever water might seep in. The idea gives Teresa a terrible thought, but she keeps it from Donna, who also has the same idea. "Auto parts," she says, instead. They begin opening boxes, idly.

"That old glass lamp you always thought was made of diamonds," Teresa says.

"The cow cookie jar." Donna removes the lid. "Nuddin'," she says, reviving a forgotten routine.

"Nuddin' but nuddin'," Teresa says, remembering.

"Nuddin' a' all."

A silence, which bothers both of them.

"They could have used this at the beach," Teresa says, opening the door of a microwave oven. Its interior is new and odorless.

"Dad always thought microwaves would kill him," Donna says, then puts a hand to her mouth.

Teresa looks at her. "I'd laugh," she says.

A problem: there are too many new boxes to fit on top of the palettes. Some things must go. So Donna pulls a few boxes from a stack. Teresa helps. The empty column reveals a wedge of space between the palettes and the back wall, a space that Teresa must investigate. She steps between the boxes and peers behind.

It is darker there, but she does not give a little cry because of this.

Donna leans over Teresa's shoulder.

Against the wall, the exercise bike, a relic, with a wide, triangular seat and pom-poms shooting from the handlebars.

A tying and untying of knots

A year before Donna will remarry—before her sons will accompany her to a new house, festooning their bedroom walls with posters she would have been embarrassed by when she was their age (a phrase that will crop up more and more regularly in her conversation, she'll notice, along with her mother's habit of saving proofs-of-purchase), before her mother makes the first of her prolonged stays, sleeping in the guest room with a portable television turned on all night, before Donna seeds the front flower beds that will be the last of her life, in this, her final home—Teresa marries.

At long last, their mother jokes.

The night of the rehearsal dinner, Donna sits with Teresa and Teresa's fiancé, Jim. This is only the second time Donna has met him, and already she feels a loose sort of kinship there: Jim, quietly funny, given to childish blushes at an off-color joke, and a habit of cupping his ear whenever someone addresses him from across the table. When Donna's boys get bored with the adults and their endless cups of coffee, begging for quarters for the video game in the restaurant lobby, Jim presents his butter knife to them, placing it atop his cloth napkin like a rare museum piece. He turns it in the light, then lowers the knife onto his lap, out of view. When he raises his hands, they are draped by the napkin.

"Please remove," he says, and Jason obliges.

Underneath, the knife rides behind Jim's intertwined fingers, levitating.

"How did you do that?" Jason says.

"He's just holding it," Matthew says.

"No, he's not."

"Don't be dumb," Matthew says, too wise for this sort of thing, Donna knows, and feels disappointed for him. When she and Teresa were little, they played a game they called "The Floating Girl," where the two of them would lie side by side in Teresa's bed, eyes closed, a thick comforter pulled above their heads, as Teresa recited an incantation. "Magic world/Find the Floating Girl," she'd say, tenting the comforter above them. After a moment, Teresa would allow the comforter to fall and Donna would feel her body rising to meet it, a little swell of magic that subsided as soon as the comforter was lifted again.

"Now you do a trick, Aunt Teresa," Jason says.

"She can't do anything," Matthew says.

One time, Teresa vanished. Donna felt the comforter descend, but no Teresa beside her. She opened her eyes. The room was dark, the air beneath the comforter close and warm. She felt her heart beating in her ears.

"Pass me a fork," Teresa says, and Matthew slides one across.

When Donna reached her hand beneath the comforter, she discovered Teresa's. Teresa allowed her to hook her fingers with hers, let her stroke the creases of her palm. Donna couldn't stop herself from holding her breath. After a while, Teresa whispered, "And now we're married."

Teresa takes the fork and cups it with both hands. She presses the sharp end to the table, then presses harder, bending the fork into an L. When she removes her hands, the fork is straight again, unharmed.

"You didn't really bend it," Matthew says.

"Y'huh," Jason says.

"No, she didn't," Matthew says. "Duh. It's just an optical illusion. We learned about it in school."

When Donna thinks of the houses left behind, she thinks of Teresa. She thinks of her in rooms with doors closed, behind every wall, in the spaces beneath floorboards. She thinks of her as just out of reach, but never really.

"Listen, honey," Donna tells Matthew, "sometimes there's no such thing."

A
Dictionary
of
Saints

———

At the end of the school year our bus driver, Captain Leroy, allowed us to hold the clunky bus microphone to our lips and make a parting speech to the other boys. The microphone was heavy, thickly corded, and gave off a whiff of electrical smoke when you pressed its square button. I tried to speak into it sideways, the way I'd seen sheriffs do on TV. "Um, everyone try and not be too weird and stuff this summer," I mumbled, "'cause that would be weird if everyone came back weird." That morning, for no real reason, I'd nearly cried double tying my Docksiders. Other mornings I'd find myself in a terrific mood, Christmas Eve happy, then realize I'd been fantasizing about wowing David Letterman with my impression of Brother Domenic, our social studies teacher. I was thirteen years old. "So, don't anybody be weird, okay?"

Our school, St. Christopher's, was run by the Brothers of the Holy Cross. I'd transferred there in the sixth grade after my brother went to live with my father. I didn't want to go to a Catholic school, but my brother, Nathan, had gone to St. Christopher's when he was my age, and my mother liked the idea. Nathan was in college now, calling me on weekends to praise campus life—a gesture, I knew, meant to suggest that I should be trying harder in school. I was a lazy student. "Do you know how many kinds of cereal they've got at the dining hall?" Nathan would say.

"How many?" I'd say, wishing we were talking about the time we found half a trombone in the weeds behind the mall, when Nathan had walked through Sears with the mouthpiece between his lips, talking like a breathy robot. I'd always thought that was the funniest thing.

"*Eight*," Nathan said. "Plus they'll make you any kind of omelet you want. Cheese, ham, mushroom, green pepper, Western. You name it."

"I'm not crazy about omelets," I said.

Nathan accidentally pushed a button. "But if you were," he said.

That afternoon we'd had an end-of-the-year party at the Brothers' house, which stood just beyond the soccer field and the rose garden, where our class, the following weekend, would graduate from eighth grade. There would be a photograph of me there, squinting above a clip-on tie, diploma in hand, blinded by the sun.

It was a magnificent house. We entered though a door that diminished to a point at its apex, like a flipped shield, and stood in a bright foyer, which opened out to a sitting room on the right and a paneled dining room on the left, the panels removable, storage spaces that were once part of the Underground Railroad, Brother Domenic explained. He removed a panel and pointed a flashlight inside. "Can you imagine, gentlemen, being asked to hide in there? The feeling of that?" We mumbled that we could not, although the idea of hiding in the walls privately excited me. I liked the idea of cracking the panel just so, spying on the brothers at the dinner table. "Terrible," Brother said.

Outside, they'd arranged a row of pizzas for us on a long picnic table, with a washtub of sodas bobbing in ice, and three kinds of salads no one bothered to touch. I spent my time hanging out with Jason Ciano and Robbie Hendricks, my two best school friends, although lately it was getting harder and harder to figure out why. Jason was newly deep-voiced and cosmically bored, and Robbie had taken to imitating him, which was like trying to sketch cinder blocks. Our friendship suddenly seemed to me a pranked elevator, stopping at every empty floor.

"Wouldn't it be funny if everyone was upside down?" Jason said, eyeing a crowd of boys locked into equally dumb conversations.

"Yeah," I said, "they'd all be like, 'What the?'"

"Yeah," Robbie said. "They'd be like, 'Whaa?'"

Jason spit an ice cube into his cup. "That'd be so completely insane," he said.

All month I'd been looking forward to the end of school, but now that it was finally here I didn't want it to happen. I wanted another month, another year to rearrange myself and become some other kind of person. The thing was, I couldn't tell how I felt about anything anymore. My allegiances were to everything and nothing at all. I performed mean, unflattering impressions of teachers whom I secretly admired and wished to be like. I was in love with wet leaves on a damp sidewalk, with the bright squares of glossy light checkerboarding the gymnasium floor, but joked that our bus smelled like Parmesan cheese. School was where I got by, joke after joke, but summer would leave me exposed, revealed. I'd sit with my friends in the shade of a pitched umbrella and have no idea what to say. I'd walk along the beach and burn my feet in the sun.

I left Jason and Robbie and went looking for the bathroom. A sleeping dog blocked the bathroom door, so I cut through the dining room, then climbed the stairs that had been in my mind all along, when I'd first seen the dog's narrow tongue sloped between his teeth. It was warmer upstairs; the windows hadn't been opened. A propped door revealed a small bedroom, bright with sun, complicated by the pattern of leaf shadows on the hardwood floor. Within this pattern, a twin bed, neatly made, and a mirrored dresser doubling the comb, aftershave, and deodorant atop it. A rubber hairbrush teetered on the edge, webbed with hair. It saddened me to think of the Brothers reading the words "Speed Stick Fresh Scent: 15% MORE — FREE!" every morning, their scalps thrilled by dirty bristles.

The bathroom door was slightly ajar. Opening it, I found Brady Carson kneeling in front of the shower curtain, sniffing a red votive candle. "They've got candles in the tub," he said. "Can you believe that?"

Brady's shirt was untucked; his hair looked like it had just been toweled. He had had only one friend at school, Michael Renge, but Michael moved away the semester before, taking whatever loan of respectability with him. There was a picture in my mind of Brady and Michael sitting across the lunch table from each other, constructing a face out of olives and crushed saltines.

"You shouldn't be snooping," I said.

"I wasn't," Brady said. "You were." He made his eyes theatrically wide. "Ooh."

Normally I would have told him to shut up, but something prevented me. "Normally I'd say shut up," I explained.

Brady ignored me. "Look." He pulled back the shower curtain to reveal a green tub rimmed with red and white candles. "They're candle crazy." He grabbed one of the largest, reddest candles—this made a wet, sucking sound—and held it to his nose. "Ah," he said, "now that's *rhazzberry!*"

After I'd washed my hands, I found Brady waiting for me in the hallway. "This hallway's haunted," he said.

"They don't want us to know about this hallway," he said.

"This hallway is strictly incognito," he said.

"I don't know what you're talking about," I said. Once, Jason had done an impression of Brady by holding his nose and squatting out a fart, which I'd laughed at like it was the funniest thing.

"Do you know about the smoking room?" Brady said. "Ooh, they don't want us to know about the smoking room." I followed him into a large sitting room with end-tabled sofas, La-Z-Boy recliners, and vinyl Barcoloungers arranged around a large console TV, on top of which lay a green hardback book, stippled like an avocado's skin, raised white letters reading A *DICTIONARY OF SAINTS*. For years, whenever I browsed a used bookstore I would make a little game out of finding that edition, but I never had any luck.

There were blankets draped across the sofas. Brady took one and put it around his shoulders. "This is them," he said, settling into one of the recliners. "This is their life." He lowered a phantom cigarette toward a domed silver ashtray, the kind I'd only seen before in bus stations and barber shops. "Pass me those salted almonds, Brother William," he said, doing a decent Brother Domenic. "I know I shouldn't, but oh well."

I took the blanket from his shoulders. "Don't," I said. The blanket smelled like menthols. "We'll get caught." I was big on not getting caught.

"It was hot under there anyway," Brady said.

"The windows aren't open," I explained.

"I could have suffocated."

"You can't suffocate if you can breathe."

"I could have combusted," Brady said. "It's a fact."

"They should open the windows."

"Everything would catch fire."

"I'm going downstairs."

"They'd think it was a cigarette that did it."

Sometimes, when I was alone, I liked to imagine explaining myself to someone who wasn't there. *The best way to open a stuck jar is to turn the jar and not your hand, see? I'm sorry about spraying this ant with glass cleaner, but he was headed for the bread drawer.* It wasn't until I returned outside and found Jason and Robbie lobbing ginkgo balls into a birdbath that I realized that's the way I'd felt upstairs, talking to Brady Carson. Like there was a third person listening. Like I was explaining myself to the kitchen countertop.

———————

My orthodontist was a short Finnish man named Dr. Kari, whose office had once been a Wendy's restaurant. Although the interior had been remodeled to look like the idea of a doctor's office—month-old *People* magazines, *Us*, *Sports Illustrated*, and *Boy's Life* leaning out from Plexiglas wall displays, conjoined chairs in alternating shades of periwinkle and ultramarine—the drive-thru window remained, which always gave me a kind of thrill.

"Does anyone ever think this place is still a Wendy's?" I asked once, before Dr. Kari could say "Wider, please, *wider*. I don't know why they can never open wider."

"Who is Wendy?" he said, then turned rubber-handled pliers just beyond my view, tightening.

"I thought this used to be a Wendy's," I explained.

"You move so I can't work," he said, then lowered a bright lamp on a swivel with a head like a show shovel, the bulb a cube of scooped ice. "Everything we do, we want to do it still, right? Please to keep still."

"Sorry," I said. Up close, Dr. Kari's nose was faintly haired, porous as a golf ball. "The window made me think so."

Dr. Kari pulled a wire from my mouth and clipped it with the pliers. "A window," he said. "What does it matter?"

My braces were a sore point with me, since all of my other friends went to Dr. Miles, the friendly, more popular orthodontist, whose braces looked like neatly quartered Chiclets, whereas mine were heinously metallic, a fence wound of X's and em dashes. My mother heard that Dr. Kari was less expensive than Dr. Miles.

"Do you know Dr. Miles?" I asked, as soon as Dr. Kari lowered a rectilinear mirror to my face: a glimpse of myself with wires shooting from my mouth like a smashed guitar.

"Never heard of him," Dr. Kari said. "Please, to keep wide. There. Better."

"Smi'uls li'ke Mi'uls," I explained. In the mirror I could see the fleshiness of my gums, and the pink rims of my eyelids. In school, I hated having to approach teachers after class, the sight of them, up close, always left me feeling a little depressed.

"We must not forget headgear," Dr. Kari said, turning the mirror away. He slid the pointy prongs into their mounts, bending them into place. "Headgear takes care of us."

When I laughed at this Dr. Kari looked at me like I was a flat tire. "Everyone just kidding," he sighed. "Everything just a joke." When he strapped the headgear into place, I felt tears in my eyes.

Two weeks after graduation I received an invitation to Brady Carson's fourteenth birthday party. A typed flyer with my name penciled between the words "We'd like to invite you, _____, to celebrate!"

"Did you get an invitation?" I asked Jason, after I'd called him with the pretense of hanging out at the mall. "Yeah," Jason snorted, "got it, ripped it, chucked it."

"Totally ducked it," I said.

"Said 'fuck it.'"

It was the same with all my friends, I learned. Each of them had gotten the invitation; each of them had thrown it away. "You're not going, are you?" Robbie asked. We were lighting clumps of dried grass with a butane lighter I'd found beneath a hydrangea bush, while Robbie's gorgeous and terribly interesting sister, Karen, luxuriated on the front lawn in a long-sleeved shirt, dark jeans, and gray athletic socks. ("People who tan for the tan miss the point," she'd explained once, widening my plans for our future like a released umbrella.)

"I don't know," I said.

"What's to know?" Robbie said. He butaned a lady bug whose safety I'd been eyeing for the past few moments. "I wouldn't go for like, three million dollars."

The day of Brady's party was hot, cloudless. My mother sat in the dining room listening to classical radio and browsing indiscriminate volumes of the *Encyclopaedia Britannica*, a summertime habit of hers that irritated me. I walked around the house sock-footed, the sense of a knock upon a door preying upon every lazily opened book, half-heard song, flipped-by TV station.

Later, I went into the dining room and sat across from my mom. "There's nothing to do," I announced.

"Is that right?" She did not look up. "I wonder why that is."

"Because everything is boring," I said.

She gave a little laugh. "That's sort of true," she said.

Getting nowhere, I went upstairs and called Nathan. We had a boring discussion about whether things were boring or not. "They'll explain that in college," he promised.

Sometimes, in Dr. Kari's chair, I felt like he was about to reveal a kind of secret to me, but I never understood this until the drive home, when my mother hummed along to oldies radio and I'd grown tired of flipping the shutters of the dashboard vents, whose center knob playfully juddered like a loose tooth. "If everything is boring," I said, "what's there to look forward to?"

"Lots of things," Nathan said.

"Like?"

"I can't tell you," Nathan said. "That'd ruin it."

Downstairs, my mom had fallen asleep. It bothered me, the idea of her sleeping. I thought of Brady's party, but there was nothing to think of, so I sat beside by my mother, hoping my sitting would wake her. "Mom?" I said. She opened her eyes, but just for a moment. Sometimes I liked the way Dr. Kari looked at me when he tightened my braces, bored but watchful, like I was a television show whose ending he'd already seen, but whose outcome might still somehow be in doubt. "Mom," I said, "do you think you could maybe drive me someplace?"

At school I'd always liked the idea of going to see the nurse, Ms. Warren, whose office door held a flaky bulletin board from its lone nail, stringed like a necklace, thumbtacked with notes, and a dry-erase board whose message was always the same: KNOCK: I JUST MIGHT BE HERE. Seeing her in the office doorway, sipping coffee from a tall paper cup, whose top made a gentle crinkling noise, gave me a kind of hope. "I don't know why they say caffeine is supposed to be so bad for you," she said one morning when I'd stopped by to see if she'd replenished the fishbowl of scratch 'n sniffs she kept just inside the door. "This morning I woke up feeling like garbage, but I'm only halfway through this coffee and already I feel like fifty bucks."

"Sometimes I can see this, like, thing, out of the corner of my eye," I said, once, when the other boys were out of earshot. For weeks I'd thought I'd been noticing something there, a trickster sunspot that ducked out of view whenever I turned to glimpse it. "It's like, this speck."

"Maybe you have a speck in your eye," Ms. Warren said. Then, "If it keeps happening, let me know. Nine hundred times out of ten, it's nothing, though." She opened her desk drawer and handed me a rare scratch 'n sniff—Motor Oil—and wrote me a hall pass. "I don't why you guys are so into those," she said, retracing her name with a chewed pen.

Once, I nearly fainted while watching a film in science class. The film was ostensibly about the ecology of the farm, live-stock, but midway though a dull account of horse feeding, a baby colt slipped from his mother's womb, slick and gelatinous as a squeezed egg. A membrane covered his bulbous eyes, which glistened when they roved within their sockets. His legs were misheld chopsticks. I raised my hand and asked to be excused, but my voice sounded strange to me, the classroom a place I hardly knew. I took a long drink from a water fountain, then let myself into Ms. Warren's office; she wasn't there. I sat back on the exam table and waited. Above me, fluorescent lights made noises like pinged glasses.

Sometimes, when no one was home, I liked to sit at the dining room table and read comic books beneath the chandeliered light, just getting into it, the formal silence, turning the pages like they were sheaves from the Gutenberg Bible. A bowl of wax fruit sat atop the table, and it was my habit to take the wax pear and roll it alongside the margin of the comic book, experimentally, until I would raise it to my lips and taste its nothing taste, like meals consumed in dreams. It was exciting to dim the chandelier, too. I liked to turn its knob until the little flickering flames trapped in-side the bulbs guttered like blown candles and then—*whoosh*—turn the knob back, a birthday wish in reverse. I mention this only to say that something of the feeling of being in the dining room greeted me each time I was alone in Ms. Warren's office, and to point out how jarring it was when Brady Carson opened Ms. Warren's door and asked me if Cathy was in.

"She's not here," I said. *Cathy!*

Brady shook his head, ruefully. "She probably had to pick up Rexy. I keep telling her she should bring him to school sometime, but Brother Richard thinks he might get into a fight with Cocoa, which seems like a long shot to me since I've never seen Cocoa do anything besides chew his collar and sleep in the oratory." Brady clicked his tongue. "I swear, it's like he's *addicted* to that collar or something."

I sat up and conjured a face that said, I know all about everything you could possibly know. Brady sat himself at Ms. Warren's desk and hunted around for a pen.

"You shouldn't go into someone else's desk," I said, but felt the advantage extend to Brady in saying so.

"Cathy doesn't mind," he said. "She's always bumming one from me anyway." He held up a thick novelty pen with a green kooshball at its point. "My parents got me this in the Amish country." He pressed a button on its side and the pen began to play "Amazing Grace." "Isn't that the stupidest thing?" Brady said. "I told them I'd never use it, but they seemed to get such a kick out of it."

"So you *gave* it to Ms. Warren?"

"Uh-huh. Well, really more of a loan, I guess." Brady tore a piece of paper from a desk pad. "Is 'salutations' with one 'l' or two?"

"Aren't you supposed to be in class?"

"Brother Richard thinks I'm in the bathroom," Brady said. "I have a very sensitive stomach. My parents wrote Brother Richard a note about it. It's spicy foods that do it. A burrito could kill me." He scribbled something at the bottom of the note. "Or even a taco." He seemed to find this haunting. "Even a taco." A few moments later he stood from the desk and moved to the doorway. "Do you want the lights off or on?" he asked. "Personally, I'd leave them off."

"Off is fine," I said.

"Nicer off. Sort of quieter."

I waited until he left, then leapt to the desk. Brady's note was pinned beneath the Amish pen. "Salutations, etc, etc," it began, in Brady's looping script. "Stopped by, but oh well. Have new idea about what we were talking about before. Hope all is swellish, etc, Brady." Then, at the bottom: "P.S.: What did the zero say to the eight?"

What did the zero say to the eight? I read the note again, then put it back. Leaving the office, I closed the door, gently, finding myself in a hallway whose emptiness seemed to press against my sides. And the pressing doubled when I opened the door again, stuffed Brady's note into my pocket, took it to the bathroom and buried it deep inside a trash can crammed with damp paper towels. At lunch I did impressions of Brother Richard until Robbie's nose bled milk.

———————

Brady's house stood at the end of a cul-de-sac, a two-story Colonial with white shutters and red trim. A wood fence marked the property line, somewhat uselessly, since Brady's lawn grew a half foot higher than the others, nurturing headless dandelions, stooped ragweed, and a green push mower frozen in its own wake of cut grass. A mailbox periscoped from a low shrub, its door open like a gasp. I walked along the driveway, where minivans and station wagons wore out-of-state plates, trying to decide whether to approach the front door or the garage, from which an orange cat now eyed me, his mouth widening into a yawn. An idea came to me that the cat was a kind of spy, but I knew this was a stupid thing to think, and I got angry with myself for thinking it.

The woman who answered the door said, "Aha, Brady's out back. Just head straight through the kitchen. Is your mother coming in, too?"

"No," I said, feeling myself blush—we'd argued in the cul-de-sac when I'd said I didn't want to go in.

"Oh, too bad. Brady thinks we need more people."

This seemed an odd way of putting things. Already I could see into the kitchen, where people who were clearly aunts and uncles, neighbors, parents were gathered around a table, talking loudly, drinking from tall plastic cups.

"Does it smell like syrup in here?" the woman said. "All day I've been thinking I've been smelling something, and now I'm thinking it might be syrup. Do you smell it, too? Well, never mind. Help yourself to a plate of whatever. There's soda in the cooler."

I made my way through the kitchen, palming two chocolate chip cookies and a carrot stick before accidentally bumping into a man balancing a tray of deviled eggs over my head. "I'm sorry, sorry," I said.

"Are you?" he said. "You don't look like a Sorry Sorry."

"He looks like a Jon," the man next to him said. "Doesn't he? Jon without the *h*."

"Are you Jon without the *h*?"

"No." I told them my name.

"He looks guilty," the second man continued. "Don't ever get caught for anything, because you look guilty. They'd see you coming, throw away the key. I don't want to insult you, but it's just a fact."

Who *were* these people? At our house, we ate birthday meals with the TV turned low; Christmas, lit candles and holiday China. Here, women shouted "Ron, don't muck your elbow in the spinach dip!"

"I've got a brother who's the same way," the second man said. "Little Lord Guiltyface. People always say, 'What's the deal with your brother?' and I tell them take a look at those eyes. That's what I say. Just like that. It's the eyes that make him look guilty."

"Plus the nose," he said.

"He's got a real handle on that mug," he said.

"Let's see your nose," the first man said, then the two of them laughed.

"What's he guilty about?" the second man said.

I wandered outside, where Brady was spraying the air conditioning unit with a garden hose. "It keeps overheating," he explained. He was wearing dress pants, shirt, and tie. A little kid with untied sneakers stood next to him, watching. "It could explode," the kid said, then danced around, gleefully.

"It could," Brady said, "or it couldn't." He narrowed his eyes. "It's simply a matter of time."

I learned that the men who'd spoken to me were Brady's uncles, the kid a cousin from Michigan, as distant to me as the moon. Everyone else: relatives, neighbors, or friends of Brady's parents.

"This is our basement," Brady said, opening its door, which was hinged like a jewelry box. Inside, wall-length shelves of old newspapers, paint cans, board games, ceramic garden figures, coiled sprinklers, a motorcycle helmet shielded like a security camera, books with titles like *The Camelot Years* and *The Story of Philosophy*, a slender puppet-show stage, folded to one side, the curtain a pillowcase scissored at the seams. "We used to have that game," I said, "Don't Lose Yer Marbles."

"The madness timer broke," Brady said. "My dad tried to use an egg timer, but."

"Not the same."

"No, it broke, too."

Upstairs we found the adults gathered inside the living room, where a movie screen had been unfurled from a T-shaped tripod. Light streaked in from spaces between heavy curtains, presently drawn by Brady's mother. The sight of a movie screen—a school object, cousin of overhead projectors, flip-top desks, and sectioned lunch trays—in someone's home impressed me as deeply as it would have been to open a station wagon's hatch and find its interior paneled with chalkboards. It was the first time I can remember feeling at home by way of school.

"Here comes the Boy Scouts," a man announced, taking sips from a tall beer. "We're saved."

Brady theatrically pumped his fists in the air, then took a victory walk around the coffee table.

"Thinks he's everything," an aunt said, a woman I'd seen earlier teasing a kitten with a deviled egg.

"That's how they are," she said.

"Runs in the family," she said.

Brady and I sat on the floor, cross-legged, eating potato chips, as the movies began. The first was greeted with applause, showing a pregnant woman standing on a grassless yard, a sprinkler fanning itself upon her bikinied body. "My mom," Brady whispered. A moment later a man appeared, bare chested, sporting a straw hat and a plastic rake. He stood next to Brady's mother and put a hand on her belly, feigning shock, surprise. "The comedian," Brady's mother said, and people laughed. "Should've hit him with the rake," someone said.

"We still have it," Brady said, but I felt like I was the only one to hear.

Next was a Christmas scene, with baby Brady swinging from an Easybaby, perilously close, it seemed to me, to a heavily tinseled tree under which presents had already been unwrapped, shorn of mystery. "Our first house," Brady said. "In Indiana." I watched him watching himself yank a xylophone along a kitchen floor. "That house was haunted," he said.

"Don't be *weird*," I said, in my best Jason, but wished the opposite. I wanted to know the secrets of the pub lamp that hung above the kitchen table like a bright gem, to plunder the refrigerator freckled with magnets, its door handle wearing a dish towel like a necktie. On-screen, Brady's mother flipped the xylophone back onto its wheels, pleasing Brady, who shrieked—noiselessly, it would turn out, for the rest of us.

"You don't want to be weird," I droned.

"Look," Brady said, pointing. A kid in a wolf mask sat a picnic table, waving flies from a limp plate of hamburgers.

"Is that you, Brady?" someone asked.

Brady nodded.

"Sure it's him. Just parts his face on a different side now."

"Is that right, Brady?" someone laughed.

"I thought he was the hamburgers."

The movie showed Brady running along a dirt path, bordered by fat trees whose roots troubled his progress. A sunspot bleached the next few frames and then Brady emerged again, this time feeding ducks along a low stone wall, where green water pooled, and paddleboats could be seen in the distance. I remembered that wall. Point Park. A place my father used to take us when we were kids, Nathan and me trailing along the banks of Point Pond, negotiating a minefield of puddles and duck dung. I remember being vaguely afraid of the lake, since I had seen—or had I really?—a watersnake sunning himself on top of a historical marker. Watching Brady ascend the wall returned the feeling of peeling off my sneakers, with their faint cucumbery dampness, and shaking them against our old station wagon, thankful to have been spared. That Point Park was a place to Brady, too, wrapped up in his experience but unknown to me, momentarily complicated my notion of the world.

"It's scary, isn't it?" Brady whispered.

I asked him what was.

"It's scary how good a climber I was," Brady said. "A spider bite did it," he said.

"Plus I touched a meteor," he said.

"But only once," he said. "I only touched one once."

"Me, too," I said, and Brady gave me a look.

"It fell into our swimming pool," I explained. "Nearly dried up all the water."

"You don't have a pool!" Brady said, delighted.

"Not after that we didn't," I said. "We couldn't after that. Who could?"

Later, Brady and I stood outside while Brady's uncles tended a dying grill, drinking beer from bright cans that Brady and I arranged into pyramids. It was starting to get dark out, cool for the first time that day. I looked up into the undersides of trees, which arched across the backyard, and did not wish to leave. After a while, one of the uncles produced a small hatchet from a dark leather bag and the other, as if the assistant in a magic show, propped a round tree stump against a concrete birdbath, laughing. Don't try this at home, the uncles said, then took turns flinging the hatchet at the stump. Sometimes they were successful; more often the hatchet winged across the yard, skipping into bushes or, thrilling to Brady and me, sticking into the side of Brady's woodshed, which made a pleasing, thunking sound. A challenge was needed to spice this dish, so the uncles said, and a playing card was affixed to the stump through some adhesive lost to memory. To this addendum a second was added: a red handkerchief that became, through the uncles' handiwork, a blindfold, pinching me behind the ears. I lifted the hatchet and tried to picture the card, a king of diamonds, enthroned at the top of the stump. The hatchet was lighter than I had imagined, and this gave me a kind of confidence, as did the knowledge that the task was impossible, preposterous. And it was the shocked cheers of the others that informed me I'd done it; I'd split the card. I would take the blindfold off and see it for myself, but for a moment I listened as one of the uncles asked Brady, "Where'd you find a friend like that?" and Brady said, "Him? He follows me everywhere."

The Knot

When JoAnne Knox saw Mo McDonough dragging Gil up her front walk, she immediately stepped away from the window and crouched behind her dresser, wondering, suddenly, if Mo could still see the top of her head. The idea both pleased and terrified her, and she giggled into the tent of her hands, but this sounded rehearsed, so she slid the phone off the dresser and called Linda Jennings instead.

"Linda, it's JoAnne. Hey, look out your front window, okay?"

"JoAnne? Why are you whispering?"

"I don't know," JoAnne whispered. "Just look outside and tell me if you see Mo McDonough coming to my door. Quick."

JoAnne heard Linda put the phone to the floor. In the background she could hear the television and the ticker tape of the Jennings' sheltie, Chester, skittering across the kitchen linoleum. When Linda returned to the phone, JoAnne thought she'd had an asthmatic attack, until she realized it wasn't Linda, but Chester nuzzling the receiver. "Christ," she said. "Fetch. Linda."

"JoAnne?" Linda said, startling her. "I'm on the upstairs phone. Oh, God, it's Mo, and she's got Gil with her. I can see them right now. Jesus, you can tell she's in a state just by looking at her."

"What's she doing?"

"She's . . . oh, she's looking in your window. Right in front of the kid."

"What's he doing?"

"He's sitting on the porch step. It looks like she's got him dressed up in a suit or something."

"The poor kid," JoAnne whispered. "She's probably got him—" she began, but at that moment the doorbell rang. "Oh, God."

A remarkable sound loosed itself from Linda's nose. "There oughta be a law," she said.

Outside, Gil pulled the untied ends of his necktie through his hands, absently, as his mother beat against the door. The small end reminded him of a hamster's tail passing through his fingers and, for a moment, he wished he had gotten some kind of pet for his birthday, instead of the black pin-striped suit he'd found draped across his bed earlier that day. He'd come home from school to find his mother sleeping at the kitchen table, still in her nurse's uniform, as ice popped unspectacularly inside a glass of ginger ale she'd forgotten on the counter. She had her arms folded beneath her head, and, looking down, Gil could see that she'd gotten herself a new pair of white nurses shoes with wide, oval-shaped buckles. Of all the things that saddened him at that moment, the newness and fatness of the buckles saddened him the most.

"You should be dressed up," she'd said, regarding him with one squinting eye. "You should be wearing a suit, so when your father gets here he'll really think it's something." She turned her head the opposite direction, and dozed again. "That's what he'll think," she said.

Gil left her and went upstairs, where the discovery of the suit was as pleasing and unsurprising as finding a quarter in the dryer. He sat next to the suit and petted the sleeves of the jacket, gingerly. "A suit," he whispered, acting out a scene in his head where his mother and father—reunited—were watching him from the doorway. "My very own suit." He plucked the tie from the shirt and draped it around his neck. The double pendulum of its ends extended well past his waist, and he wrapped them around once again, wondering if this was right. He was about to try the jacket on when the telephone rang, and he ran into his mother's bedroom, diving across the bed to intercept it before the second ring.

"Hey there, birthday boy," his father said, meaning, Gil knew, from his high, cheery tone, *I'm calling to disappoint you.* To compensate, Gil burst into a long, disjointed account of finding the suit—it was surprising to him how good he had gotten at this sort of thing—knowing that this would help put his father at ease. He told him about the tie, with its funny little stripes, and rhapsodized about the smoothness of the jacket's lining, which hid a deep, mysterious pocket he planned to stuff with action figures.

"I bet they'll like that," his father said.

"Yeah," Gil said.

"Like a sleeping bag."

"Yeah," Gil said, a little shakily, for in that moment he had felt his father to be a foolish person he did not really love, and the idea frightened him. "Like a sleeping bag."

Now, sitting on the Knoxes' front step, Gil pulled an action figure from his pocket and wondered how to break the news that his father was not coming after all. He pushed the figure's arms upward into a chin-up grip, and listened to his mother banging away at the door. Looking up, he saw a car approaching, and felt embarrassed when it slowed to pass, as the Gregory twins regarded him from the back window, then immediately ducked out of view.

Gil's mother turned to watch the car disappear around the corner. "You know," she sighed, "it's getting so hard just to be a crazy person anymore."

Gil closed his eyes, and tried to imagine himself living inside the pocket, but he knew this was silly, and he stopped imagining it.

"First, the kids stop coming on Halloween," she continued. "Then, all of a sudden, the Girl Scouts don't remember your address. Now you've got neighbors hiding from you. *Hiding.*" She gave a little laugh. "I'm telling you, it's enough to make you put the house up for sale."

"You've been saying that forever," Gil mumbled.

He could hear her new shoes groaning as she stepped away from the door. "That," she said, "is a ridiculous proposition." She moved toward the walkway and stood next to Gil. When Gil looked up, he imagined that he saw his mother the way others might have seen her, and felt a rush of embarrassment. She looked, in her various stages of dress, like someone who had appraised herself in a rear-view mirror, unaware that her long, navy raincoat —twenty years out of style if it was a day—was noticeably tight underneath the arms, and that her white nylons sagged dramatically above her too-new shoes, like two dollops of toothpaste squeezed beneath the cap.

"It's getting hard just to *be*, anymore," she whispered. "It really is." For a moment Gil was afraid she was going to cry, until she looked down at him, and he saw a change in her expression. "But your father is really going to think something when he sees that suit," she said. "That's something he won't believe." She nodded. "That's something no one will believe."

"Sure," Gil mumbled. A late afternoon breeze took the ends of his tie, slightly, and for the first time that day it began to feel a little cold outside. He returned the action figure to its pocket and hugged his arms to his chest.

His mother put a hand on his head. "Come on," she said. "We're leaving." She cupped her hands to her mouth. "Did you hear that, JoAnne?" she announced. "We're leaving."

Gil stood from the step. His mother brushed the back of his jacket, picking bits of whatever from the undersides of the sleeves.

"See?" she said, to no one in particular. "I'm being a good mother."

The Jennings' home, with its wide, windowless garage, had always reminded Gil of a fortress, and on those few occasions when he'd stood in the driveway as the door rumbled open, he had felt himself poised on the edge of something vague and spectacular. The last time he'd been there was over the summer, when he and his mother couldn't figure out how to start their push mower, and the two of them had wheeled it over to the Jennings' for an inspection. The garage had opened, majestically, and Mr. Jennings appeared from within, carrying a toolbox and a white rag, as Mrs. Jennings kept Chester at bay with a long red leash.

"Well," Mr. Jennings said, peering underneath the mower as Gil pushed on the handle, "it looks like Dan forgot to clean out the gunk at the end of last season. There's gunk caked all around the blade."

"Gunk," Gil's mother replied, sleepily. She laughed in a way Gil feared was incorrect.

Mr. Jennings chiseled away the hardened grass with a screwdriver, as Gil struggled to keep the mower steady. He could just make out the pile of gray-green clumps forming, dismally, beneath the blade, as his mother watched with a loose smile across her lips. "So much gunk," she said.

Now, as the two of them approached the front door, Gil hoped that it would be Mr. Jennings who would answer, and his disappointment was complete when he saw Mrs. Jennings part the front curtain, giving the two of them a ridiculous look of surprise, then unlocking the deadbolt and partially opening the door. "Mo," she said, putting a hand to her chest. "I thought that was you."

"It was."

"I was just getting ready to take Chester on a little walk, when I looked outside and saw you coming up the drive. And I thought, Who is this handsome young man coming up my driveway dressed in such a nice suit?"

"It's a birthday present," his mother said.

"Well, happy birthday, Gil," Mrs. Jennings said. "How old are you now?"

Gil was about to answer when Chester darted out from beneath her legs and began barking at the two of them.

"Chester!" Mrs. Jennings said. She pulled Chester by the collar, dragging him back inside. Gil moved behind his mother, hoping that Mrs. Jennings wouldn't see how frightened he was. He felt tears forming in his eyes and was suddenly angry with himself.

"I'm sorry," Mrs. Jennings said. "He gets a little feisty when he hasn't had his walk."

"That's okay, Chester," Mo said, quietly, as Mrs. Jennings tried to nudge him back inside the door. "I know you mean to say hello." She raised her arm and offered him a little wave. "I know it's getting harder and harder just to say hello anymore."

"Oh, he's bad," Mrs. Jennings said, closing the door. Chester moved to a low window and put his nose to the glass, growling. "I really *should* be taking him on a walk," she continued, giving a sharp click of the tongue. Gil noticed that she kept one hand on the doorknob, turned.

"We were wondering if you could help us," Mo said, a statement. "Dan's coming to take Gil out to dinner, and we don't know how to tie his tie." She stepped aside to afford a full view of Gil in his untied tie. "I figured someone would know," she explained.

Mrs. Jennings clapped her hands together. "Is *that* what this is all about? Oh, Mo," she said, "his *tie*." She gave the two of them a bemused look, then stepped from the door, taking the ends of the tie and wrapping them once around each other. "Well, let's see," she said. "I think it's twice around, then down through the middle and—" she shaped the knot into a lopsided square, then pulled it toward the collar. Gil could see that the small end was longer than the wide, and that the entire tie curved inward from the knot down, looking like a tongue tasting a lemon wedge.

"Well, that's not right, is it?" Mrs. Jennings said, undoing the knot and starting over again. "Maybe it's once around, then up and through, then around again." She stopped and put a hand to her mouth. "Do you know, I can't remember." Her voice drifted to a remote key. "I honestly can't remember. Isn't that terrible?"

"Oh," Mo said, "a lot of things are terrible. I bought Gil a nice birthday cake last night, and now I can't find it. Can you believe that? A birthday cake." She shook her head. "Terrible."

A strange silence settled upon the three of them as a car passed in the distance. Gil watched the two women, happy to note a similarity in their expressions—his mother with her lips drawn tightly together, Mrs. Jennings with her hand on her chin—as if whatever it was that accounted for their silence might be the exact same thought. The idea pleased him.

"Maybe you left it in the car?" Mrs. Jennings said. "Sometimes I forget groceries in the corners of the trunk."

"I'm afraid of the trunk," Mo replied. "Besides, I remember taking the cake inside and hiding it somewhere. I just can't find it."

And this was the truth. After talking to his father, Gil returned downstairs to find his mother standing on a kitchen chair, digging through the cabinet above the refrigerator. She pulled out item after item—an empty coffee tin, an unopened box of Christmas napkins, two weedy serving baskets—as Gil went around the room, closing all of the cabinet doors she'd left open.

"Useless," Mo whispered. She banged one of the baskets against the top of the refrigerator. "I'm useless." She put her hands to her face, accidentally knocking one of the baskets off the side. Gil went to retrieve the basket and offered it to his mother, who took her hands from her face and regarded him with a surprised expression.

"You found your suit," she said. "Oh, just look at you, would you? I mean, just *look* at you."

Gil smiled and performed a little modeling spin, knowing this would please her.

"Your father won't believe it. But he's going to have to," she added, "he's going to have to believe it."

Gil handed her the basket. "Yeah," he said. "He's going to have to."

———

Gil followed his mother through the Jennings' backyard, observing the shavings of cut grass sticking to his new dress shoes. In a little while they would need to hop the Gregorys' hedge, and Gil prayed that the Gregorys wouldn't be looking. He very much wanted to be done with this, to be home again, where he could figure out a way to break the news to his mother, and the thought of another encounter depressed him. Ahead, he watched his mother lift her skirt and hop the hedge, Mo laughing as the zipper of her raincoat caught a twig in its teeth.

"Oh, hello," she said, and for a moment Gil thought she was addressing the twig, until he hopped into the yard and saw the Gregory twins—Pete and Roy—staring back at him. They were standing around a running garden hose, nozzle down in the muddy lawn, as a plume of brown water percolated above the surface. Pete, the skinnier one, had the guiltiest face Gil had ever seen, and Roy's wasn't much better—he made a lame attempt to stand in front of the hose as soon as he saw them.

"We're drowning the devil," Roy explained.

Mo moved closer to the gurgling hose and clapped her hands together. "Well, it's about time," she said. "Somebody had to."

The twins nodded, nervously, as the four of them watched the water as if it were a campfire. Gil didn't mind the Gregory twins seeing them: they were too young to really worry about, and didn't have many friends besides each other. "I'll bet he's drowning," Gil said, and Roy squeaked in agreement.

"Uh-huh," Pete said.

After a while, Roy looked at the two of them and said, "How come our mom's scared of you?"

Pete pushed him, and Roy tried to grab Pete's shirt.

"Oh, it could be a lot of things," Mo offered. "It's getting hard for people not to be afraid of everything anymore. I know I'm afraid to drive at night. And of parades."

The twins released each other—Pete had Roy by the sleeve—and looked to Gil for some kind of explanation. Gil met their eyes and realized that they were afraid. A silence was broken when Roy muttered, "You're wearing a suit."

"Yeah," Gil said.

Roy prodded the hose with his shoe. "That's dumb," he said.

As long as Gil could remember, the Pattersons had been his parents' friends. Gil's father, especially, had been close with Mr. Patterson, who often watched basketball games with him in the downstairs study, while Gil sat in the living room, pressing the pedals of a Baldwin grand, mystified by the yawning of the hammers within. His mother sat on the back deck with Mrs. Patterson and Colleen, the Pattersons' college-aged daughter, Mo doing all the talking, as the other women made knowing, understanding nods, and laughed at things Gil supposed must be funny. He liked to hover about their conversations, hoping for some kind of acknowledgment from Colleen, who drove a Mustang convertible, and whom he had once accompanied on a last-minute cigarette run, the sense of their mission and the white noise of wind combining to make him just a little bit in love with her.

After his parents' separation, though, it seemed that the Pattersons had disappeared. True, he sometimes saw Mrs. Patterson driving her white sedan up the main drive, but, even when he offered a little wave, her eyes looked past him, and the person behind the wheel seemed to him someone he no longer knew. He watched the car disappear around the corner, wishing for things he could not name.

Now, standing in the Pattersons' driveway, he watched his mother peer into the window of a brown station wagon, which was parked against the garage. There were half-moons of rust around the wheel wells and a vacuum cleaner hose slung across the backseat.

His mother stepped away from the car and gave a long, low whistle. "Things must be getting hard for the Pattersons, too," she said, and Gil thought he detected a sob in her voice. It was clear that the walk had tired her out more than usual, and she leaned against the car, placing her hands on the hood. Gil saw that her new white shoes were now grass stained and muddy, and for the first time that day he was truly afraid—afraid that he'd been wrong to mislead her, afraid that the truth was coming, and that the truth would kill her. "Mom," he mumbled, knowing she was too far to hear.

She moved from the car to the front door and rang the bell.

The door opened, partially, then jerked back on a security chain. Near the bottom of the opening, the face of a little boy appeared. "I'm not supposed to open the door," he said. "But I did."

Behind him, the sound of a woman's voice could be heard. "Darnell! Get away from that door!"

"Uh-oh," Darnell said.

A moment later Darnell was whisked away, and the chain removed, as the door swung open to reveal a woman dressed in gray sweatpants and a long-sleeved T-shirt, the sleeves rolled to the elbows. "I'm sorry," she said, "how can I help you?"

"You have no idea," Mo said, then laughed.

The woman looked at Gil, who managed to ask if the Pattersons were home. The woman told them that they were away for the week, and that she was the housekeeper, and would be glad to leave a note if they wished.

"You are so helpful," Mo said. "I mean that. I really, really do." She looked as if she'd forgotten that the woman was standing there at all, and Gil lowered his head in embarrassment. "It's getting harder and harder for people just to be helpful to one another. It really is."

"Isn't that the truth?" the woman said. "It's a messed-up world anymore." She looked at Gil and, in an instant, did something he did not expect: she winked. "I was just telling Darnell not to go answering the door when I heard you ringing, and then I saw you through the window and saw what nice-looking people you were, and I thought, Now what am I doing getting so upset over two nice people knocking at the door?"

"Oh, it's true, it's true," Mo said. Then, "The Gregory boys were afraid of us, too."

"Isn't that awful?" the woman said. "And you two being so nice."

Darnell, who'd been hiding behind his mother's leg, poked his head out and said, "Your clothes are messy."

His mother crouched down, whispered something sternly in his ear, and nudged him back inside.

"Oh," Mo said, looking down at Gil's shoes and slacks, which were both spotted with mud. "And his father is coming to take him to his birthday dinner," she said, then broke down in tears. "And I can't find the cake." She knelt to the ground and tried rubbing out the spots of mud, which only smeared across the fabric.

"Mom," Gil said. "Don't. It's okay. It's okay."

"His daddy's coming to take him to dinner?" the woman said, leaning down with Mo. Mo nodded.

"We'll get him ready," the woman said. She helped Mo to her feet, and lead the two of them inside. "I promise."

She told Gil to go into the laundry room and take off his shoes, while she sat Mo on the living room sofa and talked with her awhile. Gil could hear his mother crying, as the woman comforted her, saying "I know exactly what you mean," and "You're right about that, you're absolutely right." When he entered the laundry room he found Darnell inside, racing toy cars inside an open dryer. He was embarrassed to have Darnell watching him, but he took off his shoes anyway and shook them over the sink.

"Is your mom crazy?" Darnell said.

"I dunno."

"How come?" he said, but Gil couldn't tell if he meant how come she was crazy, or how come he didn't know. He turned the water on and carefully ran the heels under the faucet.

Darnell gave a little laugh. "You're scared of me, aren't you?"

"No," Gil lied.

"Yeah you are," Darnell said. "You're scared."

Gil was about to respond when Darnell's mother walked in and yelled at him for playing with the dryer. She picked him up by his arm and said, "Don't tell me you need an attitude adjustment, or I'm gonna adjust it with the back of my hand." Darnell made a pouty face as she led him out of the room and closed the door behind him.

"Now," she said, "let's see if we can get you all fixed up." She pulled out a wooden step stool, and had Gil stand on it. "You shouldn't have been out there walking through the grass," she began, but she had barely touched a cloth to Gil's leg, when he put his face in his hands and burst out, "Don't let her know that no one's coming. *Please.*" He could feel himself trying to wipe away tears, but his fingers were dumb little fish at the ends of his hand, and he felt an awfulness arise within his stomach. "She's going to be so upset," he said.

The woman put a hand to his head. "Listen," she said, "we're not going to say anything that's going to upset her. You understand me?"

Gil wiped his eyes and tried to imagine himself living inside the pocket. "She's going to be sooo upset," he said. "I should never have. Never."

"Listen to me," the woman said. She took his hands in her own and crouched down to meet his eyes. "We're not going to say *anything* that's going to upset her, okay?"

Gil tried to wipe his nose across his arm.

"Tell me," she said. "What's the thing we're not going to say?"

Gil looked at her, and, for a moment, it was like living inside the pocket. "Anything that upsets her," he said.

"That's right," she said, and wiped his face with the cloth. "That's the thing we're never going to say."

After she had cleaned him up, she took the ends of the tie in her hands and expertly tied a Windsor knot. Gil was fascinated by the folding of the ends over and around each other, and by the solidity of the knot beneath his chin. "There," the woman said.

Gil buttoned his jacket, and hopped off the stool. "There," he said.

They found Mo asleep on the sofa, hands tucked underneath her head, as Darnell sat on the piano bench, watching. "She's asleep," he said, a little too loudly, and Mo turned the other way.

"Don't," the woman mouthed, and put a finger to her lips.

"I know," Darnell whispered.

Gil sat next to her, and put a hand on her shoulder. "Mom," he said. "I'm ready." When she looked up, Gil could see pink cushion-marks across her cheek. She blinked at him and gave way to a smile.

"Oh, Gil," she said. "We're going to make him believe."

Outside, it was now nearly dark as the two of them arrived home. Gil pried the garage door open with a garden tool (his mother had broken a key in every lock) and turned on the interior lights, saddened to see the sight of baskets still on top of the refrigerator, the cabinet door swung wide. He pulled a chair to the refrigerator and put the baskets away, then closed the door, softly.

"The cake," his mother said. "I'd forgotten about the cake." She looked at him as if he were proctoring an exam, then moved to the family room and sat on the sofa. "What a stupid thing," she said, absently.

Gil put the chair back, and watched his mother curl up on the sofa. "Dragging you around the neighborhood," she mumbled. "Stupid." Gil went into the room and sat next to her. "Don't say that," he whispered.

"It's true," she said, and her voice caught, suddenly, horribly. "I'm a stupid, stupid person." She put her face in her hands. "I'm crazy," she said.

Gil pulled her hands from her face and held them in his own. "Don't say you're crazy," he said. His voice was a stretched band. "Ever."

She looked at him, disbelievingly, then turned away. "It's true," she said.

Gil tightened his hold on her hands. "Listen," he said. "That's the thing we're never going to say anymore. Understand?"

She didn't respond.

"Tell me," he said. "What's the thing we're never going to say?"

She turned to look at him and he knew. He knew how he looked to her, in his new jacket and striped tie, all knotted and nice. He looked okay saying it and he knew it.

"That I'm crazy," she whispered.

"That's right," he said. He took a blanket from the end of the sofa and draped it over her, carefully, making sure it covered her stocking feet. "That's right."

When he left the room, he could hear the heavy sound of her breathing, heartbreaking and steady.

———

Upstairs, Gil took off his dress shoes—he was startled by how good this felt—and searched his bedroom closet for the right kind of hanger to hang dress pants on. He knew the kind he needed— wood, with a funny metal bar across the middle—and went into the guest room closet to find one. The room had been the one his father had lived in during his last few weeks in the house, and a few of his things remained. Gil opened the closet door, setting off a chime of hangers within, and peered inside.

High on the top shelf, wrapped in thin, translucent grocery bags, was the veiled shape of a birthday cake.

Gil reached underneath the wrappings and lowered the cake to his chest. Through the opening of the bags, he could just make out the lettering of his name and the blue haze of confectionery flowers around the border. "The cake," he said, imagining a scene in which his mother was watching him from the door. He could feel a nervousness inside his stomach.

Downstairs, Gil placed the cake on the kitchen table and slid the bags away. He looked into the family room to see if this had woken his mother, but she did not move. Gil sat at the table and turned the cake toward him, reading its blue, loopy lettering like it was a kind of puzzle he was about to solve. Then he turned the cake the other way, facing it out toward the family room, and positioned himself behind it, neatly, in the arrangement that would be most pleasing to his mother.

He folded his hands and waited.

Be
True
to
Your
School

J,

Well, I finally got the last e-mail you sent me. Sorry it took me so long to get back to you. They only let us use the "lab" three days a week now (I don't know why they call it that) since the seniors complained that the underclassmen were hogging all the "lab time." They keep saying we're going to get more computers, but who knows? It still smells like Band-Aids in here, in case you were wondering.

Okay, it's been two days since I wrote that last paragraph. Sorry. I had to close out of e-mail because like, three million people came in and started using the lab for no apparent reason. Plus I kept deleting the paragraph that used to go here. It was about how guilty I feel when I make fun of people (like Liz) even though it's the only way I seem to make friends anymore. Do you ever feel that way? I mean, that's the way we became friends, when you think about it. Making fun of everything.

I want to change. But how? Plus I still get angry. Like when you told me about all your new friends in Florida, and I didn't write back for like, two weeks. I'm such a baby. Sometimes I can't believe you're still friends with me.

Some senior just sat next to me. Right now he's saying, "Rob, give me one of those, man . . . no, I didn't. YOU did." Now he's opening a Hershey's Kiss.

Did I tell you that my mom had to get surgery for that mole on her neck? I went with her to the hospital. She wasn't even nervous. She kept making jokes about stuff. We heard that commercial for Rogie's Steakhouse on the way over and she kept doing the little pig grunt they do at the end, remember? I mean, it is pretty funny, but come on. I was too nervous to even crack a smile.

I felt better in the waiting room. You wouldn't believe how nice they've made waiting rooms these days. It had this plush sofa with tiny green pillows that was more comfortable than our sofa at home. It was like the nicest sofa I've ever sat on. Seriously. Plus they still had a Christmas tree in the corner (real) with fake gifts underneath (I tested) and all these nice brass ornaments and blinking lights doing their thing for no one but me. I just sat with a stack of magazines across my lap and really got into it. The lights and the sofa and the magazines. Don't make fun of me for saying this, but I felt like I was going to cry. Right there in the waiting room. Then my mom came out with this huge, square bandage on her neck, smiling like nothing was out of the ordinary and all of the sudden I was mad at her. Like she'd ruined my little Christmas. I didn't even talk to her on the drive back.

God, I can't believe I just wrote that! I didn't mean it like that. I meant—I don't know what I meant.

J,

Thanks for writing back so soon. I feel less terrible now. *Danke.* Yes, I know exactly what you mean about haircuts. I feel the same way. Like I'm on display. All that looking at yourself in the mirror. I get nervous. Same thing happens to me at nice restaurants when the waitress has to recite all the specials. Where are you supposed to *look*?

Too bad about your sailboat (I can't believe you have a sailboat). Maybe you can spend the winter fixing it up? Ooh, then there could be a Big Race between you and the Rival Sailboats. Your crew would be a bunch of underdogs, determined to hold together against incredible odds, fighting to speed ahead of the Rival Sailboats . . . (okay, I'll stop).

Did I tell you?—I ended up going over to Liz's the other night. It was weird. We didn't seem to have much to talk about anymore. She's got this new habit of closing her eyes when she says something she thinks is significant. I don't know when this started. Like, she told me how Mr. Berg wrote some encouraging comments to her on her last English paper. "He told me this was one of the best papers he's ever read," she said, (OPEN), "and, he said," (CLOSED) "he can assure me he's read quite a few." I wanted to put my arms around her and say "Come back, Liz," but I didn't. I told her that was great. She closed her eyes and said, "Thanks."

Her parents are still the same. Mrs. Lawrence was as frantic as ever. She kept going on and on about you being in Florida. "Oh, what will they do without Jennifer?" she said, then hugged me and kept saying it. "What will they *do*?" (Remember the time she thought there were mice living inside their Christmas tree? I've always sort of loved her for that.) Mr. Lawrence still parts his hair in the middle. He shook my hand like I'd won a prize.

They just got a DVD player, so we ended up watching a movie with her parents and Toby. *Jurassic Park II*—ugh. There was so much stuff to make fun of, but I couldn't say anything about it because of her parents being around, but God, was it awful. Like all the dinosaurs were sooo overdone, all these ridiculous details that were supposed to make you think "Wow, how lifelike!" when all it was was a bunch of drooling and blinking. I don't know much about dinosaurs, but personally I don't think they drooled all over everything or spent the greater part of their day blinking like they'd just been poked in the eye. (You would have loved this one moment when Toby kept freeze-framing Jeff Goldblum's face

over and over, saying, "*I'm Jeff Goldblum and nobody cares!*"
until Mr. Lawrence told him to cut it out. Sometimes I swear the
only person in that family who gets what's funny is Toby. The
poor kid.)

Anyway, after that we hung out in Liz's room for a while. Liz
showed me pictures of this guy she met last summer, Glen. Has
she told you about him? He sort of looks like a cookie jar. I mean,
he's not fat or anything, but he has this glazed, peaceful look,
like he wouldn't mind if someone came along and pulled a pecan
sandie out of his head. He wears wire-rimmed glasses: —o-o—.
Hobbies: likes to play his acoustic guitar in the mountains (I main-
tained a straight face) and write poems in cafés. "Villanelles," Liz
said, and closed her eyes.

Later she showed me some e-mails he'd sent her. I sat next
to her and pretended to laugh whenever Liz read something she
thought was clever. I mean, some of it was sort of funny (at least
he makes fun of things), but most of it was him just talking about
himself. Plus he uses all that dumb e-mail abbreviation you know
I hate, like "how r u?" and "what's nu w u?"

I sat there and got angry. But not because of Glen. I was mad
at Liz. And I was mad at myself. I don't know how to explain it.
I was mad that we were reading e-mail from a boy, thinking that
was a fun thing to do. Then I was mad at myself for being mad at
myself, since that's one of the things I've been trying to fix about
myself lately, along with not making fun of everything.

But I couldn't help being angry. I wanted to stand up and
say "This is stupid, Liz. Let's go downstairs and play pool with
Toby," but I couldn't. I wasn't supposed to want that. I'm supposed to want mooning over boys. I wondered if Liz felt the
same way.

Do you know what I mean?

It's like this: Remember when Liz used to carry an aluminum
foil "vase" inside her lunchbox, stuffed with dandelions? How
she'd put it on her lunch tray for "atmosphere"? God, Liz used
to be so funny sometimes. That's what I wanted to say to her. I
wanted to say, "Liz, Glen has no idea who you really are, because
Glen doesn't know about the aluminum-foil dandelion vase." But
she wouldn't have gotten it. She would have just thought I was
being overcritical (her word for me) and told me to grow up (I

HATE when people say this). But the truth is, Liz was more Liz in sixth grade. I was more me in fifth.

Fifth Grade Forever!

My new slogan. No, my new slogan is—I don't know what my new slogan is.

I've got to keep myself from re-reading these when I'm done. I always want to delete them. A bad sign. I barely mean anything I say. Really. If anyone else is reading this I'd just like to say that Liz Lawrence is a fantastic human being full of love, sympathy, and kindness and I am a total whiner. So there.

One last thing: next week is Spirit Week.

Adios.

J,

Report in Real Time:

I'm writing to you. A senior to my left (boy) is reading his e-mail. Now he's typing. He can't type.

The moment before I started my "report" he came in and sat next to me. (I was writing you an e-mail about Mr. Embry's new "deluxe" chalk set.) He looked over and said, "Great American novel?" Bad joke, I know, but it made me embarrassed somehow. So I closed out of e-mail and started surfing Amazon instead.

He opened his book bag. He took out a pen, a notebook. Then he fished out a Ziplock of dried apricots and put them between us. They looked like tiny, gnarled fingers.

"Want some?" he said.

I took two (but didn't call him in the morning, ha, ha, he, etc.). I said something clever like, "I've never had a dried apricot before." He said some thing understanding like, "Oh." I ate my apricot. He ate his apricot. We didn't say anything. He went to Yahoo Sports. I scrolled for negative customer reviews of *The Country of the Pointed Firs*. (These are really funny, by the way . . . here's one . . .)

> *Let's Build a Time Machine . . .*
> Reviewer: *Jason*, from <u>Skokie, IL.</u>
> I, along with many unfortunate AP students, was forced to read this for summer reading. I found it pointless, stupid, and a total waste

of nine dollars. Nothing happens, unless looking for herbs and thinking about pine trees 24/7 counts. Thank god we also had to read *The Time Machine,* which wasn't all that great either, but at least it wasn't 150 pages about making "spruce beer." *The Country of the Pointed Firs* made me wish that *I* had a time machine so I could go back in time and tell myself not to be born so I wouldn't have to read this.

I thought about showing it to the senior, but didn't. I tried to look at him without really looking. I'm sort of good at that. He had a watch on, but not a "cool" watch, which you know I hate. It looked like something someone's dad would wear. Gold and clunky. I liked it.

After a while he said, "It's funny."

I said what was?

He said, "It's funny how we're eating dried apricots."

!?

Pretty good thing to say, huh? What do you think?

Okay, he just stood up. Okay, I just toggled back to this e-mail. I'm going to go now, but please write back and let me know if you think I'm being dumb. Have you ever had dried apricots? They're sort of not bad. Chew-ee.

This wasn't in real time after all, I guess.

———— ————

J,

It was good to finally talk to you last night. Now I have nothing to say. My cupboard has been emptied. *Wah!*

In the meantime, here's that e-mail I never sent you (the one about Mr. Embry). Friday we're having Spirit Assembly. You know how I get about Spirit Assembly.

Hope all is swell—K.

. . . Mr. Embry's wife gave him a deluxe chalk set for his birthday. It's this long tin that opens like a container of Altoids. Inside there are two rows of colored chalk, rainbowlike. You can tell he's sort of nervous about using it. (He's still nervous about everything. The other day he blushed so hard I thought he might pop. He was taking attendance and asked if anyone had seen Cathy Nyberg, and Jenna Purvis said, "Yeah, I saw her in the bathroom a few minutes ago. She said she'd be a little late. I think it's, you know, that time of the month." Mr. Embry nearly stapled his tie to the roll book.)

Anyway, he has this new habit of standing in front of the room with the chalk tin in hand like a painter's palette, trying to decide which color to use. It takes him forever.

"Now, for line A-B," he'll say, "I'll use, let's see, ultramarine." Then he'll draw his ultramarine A-B across the board, making it nice and straight.

Sometimes, from the back of the room, Larry Webb will say "That's a beautiful color, Mr. Embry." But Mr. Embry will just ignore him. "Now, for tangent G-B," he'll say. "I think I will try—"

"Magenta, Mr. Embry," Larry says. "Make it magenta."

Yesterday Mr. Embry was drawing a triangle when Larry started up again. "Ochre, Mr. Embry, I'm feeling a little ochre this morning." Mr. Embry stopped drawing, but he kept his hand to the board. I could see the tension in his knuckles. I could see the places where his sportcoat was threadbare.

"Larry," he said. "Would you please stop making fun of the colored chalk?" He paused. "I'm getting a little tired of it."

"I'm sorry, Mr. Embry," Larry said. "I just thought ochre might look festive."

I felt my breath get stuck in my chest. I wanted something to happen. But nothing happened. Mr. Embry finished the triangle and class was over.

But here's the thing: today Mr. Embry came in all happy. Chipper. He made a joke about everyone looking sleepy. He sipped from this gianormous coffee cup. He didn't take attendance.

Then he started his lesson plan. He picked a piece of broken chalk from the board and drew the first figure, naming all the different points, circling this and underlining that. The same chalk that's been sitting there since forever, all white and crumbly. After a while, he set the chalk down and stepped back from the board. "And that's what I love about geometry," he said, and gave us this embarrassing smile. We could see him start to blush. No one asked him what he meant (thank God).

After class, I lingered for a while, wanting to say something to him, but I couldn't think what. Mr. Embry sat at his desk and separated papers into little piles. His ears were red, raw looking. I went up to the desk, but turned away. I left the room and hurried to lunch. But I couldn't stop thinking about it. I'm still thinking about it.

What was it I thought I was going to say?

J,

Me and My Mom at the Pathmark Express Checkout Register, Last Night, Around 8 p.m:

Me: We shouldn't have gotten two Ben and Jerrys.

Mom: You're right. Do you want to grab a third?

Me: We eat too much crap. That's why we're always tired. (I point to a *Fitness* headline: 10 HIGH-ENERGY EATS — RAW!)

Mom: Chunky-Monkey is number seven.

Me: I'll meet you outside.

Mom: I think we picked the slowest lane.

J,

That's funny about your brother being afraid of mylar balloons. Is this a new thing? You'd think I'd remember something like that. In a way I kind of see his point. They're a little creepy.

I don't know if I ever told you this, but one time my mom got one from her coworkers that was in the shape of the Energizer bunny. It had words across the bass drum: "Congrats to Someone Who Keeps Going and Going!" Anyway, she brought it home and let it float around the house for a while. It bugged me. Sometimes it would be at the top of the stairs, bumping its ears against the hallway light, making this sound like cellophane unballing inside a trash can. I wanted to pull it down and pop it with scissors (I couldn't reach). Once it floated into the kitchen when I was alone and I got so freaked I called Liz and ended up talking about cell phones. Liz: cell phones hurrah! Me: what was wrong with carrier pigeons?

Anyway, after a few days it started hovering at eye level. I wanted my mom to throw it out. I wanted her to say, "Isn't this the ugliest thing?" But she didn't. She was real quiet all week and didn't say much of anything. Sometimes she went to bed before me and I'd be alone in the living room with the balloon, me watching Letterman and the balloon crinkling above the heating vent. I moved it to the dining room and let it do its creepy thing in there instead.

But here's the thing: a few days later I found the balloon in the trash can, folded like a T-shirt. I fished it out and unfolded it. *Congrats to Someone Who Keeps Going and Going!* I put it on the kitchen table and tried to smooth away the folds. Didn't work. But I kept trying. I got this feeling. I felt like the balloon was a piece of skin I'd made my mom throw away (this sounds so stupid, I know). But that's what it was like. Skin. It felt all wrinkly and slick. So I tucked it into my book bag and carried it upstairs. I hid it inside an old shirt box and buried it in the back of my closet.

It's still there, I guess. I'll show it to you next time you visit, if you want. I know how you love stuff like that.

The other night my mom said, "Don't try to fit everything into one lifetime. Save a little for the next." We were watching some old war movie on PBS that had put us both to sleep. When I asked her what she meant, she said, "I didn't say anything."

What do you think that means?

J,

Thanks for telling me about your house. I like the way you described it. That's weird, you having your own bathroom. I've always wondered what that would be like. Don't feel bad about liking the wallpaper. (I can see it, by the way, all those little scenes—I'm picturing those old newspaper-ad tabletops they used to have at Wendy's. Is this close?) I know what you mean about liking things a little bit ugly. I can't feel comfortable in a place unless it's got some crappiness to it. I've always kind of had a thing for those stupid wall sconces we have in our family room (the ones that look like seashells). Sometimes I turn them down low and lie on the sofa with that pink-and-black afghan across my feet. I can get into that.

I think that's why I don't like Liz's new house as much. I mean, it's nice, but there's no place that isn't. I think that's why I like hanging out in the basement instead, playing pool. Because the basement is a little grungy, with all those patio chairs stacked behind the water heater and all Liz's old crap spilling out of boxes, like that science ribbon she won in third grade for making her Venus fly trap go vegan. I always look for that.

I stayed over last weekend. Liz's parents were having a party. Liz and I were supposed to be "bartenders," but all we did was hand people cups and napkins. I tried to talk to Liz about Mr. Embry, but she didn't get it. "Isn't he a geek?" she said. "I can't believe he's married. Could you imagine being married to Mr. Embry? I couldn't."

"That's not what I mean," I said.

"What do you mean then?"

"It's something else," I said, but left it at that.

That night I slept on Liz's floor, trying to think what it was. It got late. I heard people laughing downstairs and my thoughts got all mixed in with that. I couldn't even tell what I was thinking.

Sometimes I think I have no idea about anything. Write back and tell me you know what I mean so I can feel okay again. Or just write to me about your sailboat. I can't get enough of that sailboat.

J,

My mom got her bandage off last night. We went out for pizza afterward, to celebrate (her idea). She wanted to go to Pappy's, but I freaked out because I know too many people who work there, so we ended up going to Pizza Hut instead, where our waiter turned out to be Dennis Schroeder. Go figure.

My mom told me stories about work. Sometimes these can be pretty good, but most of the time they make me sort of depressed. I don't know why. Like she was telling me about someone who taped a photocopy of something funny to someone else's monitor and the whole thing just made me mad. Then she kept repeating the punchline because I guess I wasn't laughing, and that made me even madder.

"Something the matter?" she said.

I told her no.

"Doesn't look like a no."

I told her to forget about it. We ate in silence. Sometimes she would turn her head to watch the TV in the corner and I would see the mark on her neck where the mole used to be. You could see where they'd patched the skin together. This faint, pinkish scar. I sat there watching her laugh at whatever was on, and I got this terrible feeling. I felt guilty for everything. I wanted to tell her I was glad she was okay, but I just ended up getting mad at her again. I didn't say a word.

I'm sick of being mad at everything. Oh, I am, I am!

I'm going to go spin my locker combination lock until I feel better. Sometimes that helps.

Later days, K.

_____

J,

Today we had Spirit Assembly (I missed the bus to write you this—it's 2:50 already). They still hold it in the gym, like always. And they still let Mr. Berg be the emcee, although you'd think they would have figured out by now that he's the last person who should be emcee. The first thing he did was throw a basketball into the air, telling us to yell "Go!" every time it hit the ground. That lasted for about two bounces. Embarrassing.

I was glad to be in the gym, though. You know how much I like it there. They're still redoing the floor and "upgrading" the bleachers. I don't know why. I like the old bleachers. I like the old floor with that awful tiger painting that looks more like Garfield (your joke). They took down those block letters that used to be above the locker room entrance, but you can still see where the words once were, ghostly white against the newer paint: BE TRUE TO YOUR SCHOOL. I love how that's still there. It made me stupid happy to see it again.

I sat next to Liz. She kept making fake hooting noises every time Mr. Berg asked us who had spirit, cupping her hands to her mouth and letting him have it. That's what everyone was doing. Faking. The guys behind me were stomping the bleachers so hard I could feel my teeth rattle. They kept laughing, making jokes about how stupid everything was. When the mascot came out, one of them stood up and shouted, "I love you T. T. Tiger!" and then his buddy screamed, "In a more-than-friends way!" Everyone was getting into it. "Be my lover, T. T. Tiger!," someone else called out. "You complete me, T. T. Tiger!"

I sat there and watched Liz. Her face was red from laughing. "Oh, my God," she said. She looked at me as if to say, Isn't this hysterical? and I gave her this big laugh. Because that's what I was doing. Laughing. I couldn't help myself. I felt like the air was shutting off around me.

Then the marching band came marching through the locker room doorway. They burst through a paper "wall" with the words "Roast The Hawks!" on it. But the wall didn't break at the top, and it knocked their hats off as they passed through. I watched them, and felt tears in my eyes. I wiped one away before Liz could see. I could hear her saying things to me, but it was like her words were handfuls of broken glass. I couldn't do anything with them. I looked at her and it was like I wasn't sure if I was laughing anymore.

I must have pushed by her and made my way to the end of the bleachers. I must have jumped down and made it to the exit, because I remember thinking that I was about to feel a hand on my shoulder and a voice telling me to stop. But I didn't. I went out into the hallway, where the marching band sounded like a train passing in the distance.

I walked to the computer lab. The door was locked, but not shut all the way. Inside, the lights were off. I left them that way. I sat down and started writing to you. I deleted what I wrote, because it didn't make any sense. I missed you so much. And I missed Liz. I missed my mom, too, really bad. I couldn't stop thinking about her. I felt like I'd been this horrible person all along, and that everyone else was fine, that Liz was fine, and my mom was fine, and the problem was me. I couldn't get my legs to stop shaking (they're still a little weird right now). But I sat and wrote this to you even though it doesn't make sense. I'm tired of not making sense.

I'm going to go now—someone just came in and turned the lights on. Bye.

J,

Thanks for calling. You'll be glad to know my weekend turned out not so bad after all. My mom and I went to this nature preserve where you were supposed to be able to see some rare kind of woodpecker. (She read about it in the paper. The Weekend section is the closest we usually get to nature.) It was weird. We sat in this little wooden hut (bird blind) and waited for woodpeckers to show up outside this long, narrow window. But all we saw were birch trees with heavy birdfeeders tied to their branches. We were alone, watching the branches dip and bend in the breeze. It got a little cold.

"Mom," I said. "What do you think about when you're at work?"

"Easy," she said. "Lunch." She hummed the *Woody Woodpecker* tune.

"No," I said, "seriously."

She looked at me. "Why?"

"I don't know," I said. "I kind of want to know."

So she told me. It was strange. It was all about me, whether I'm happy, whether I'm lonely, whether or not she's being a good mom. Stuff like that. "I think about coming home," she said. "A lot." We sat that way for a while, not saying anything. No birds appeared. Nothing. It was like I could hear the tiniest creaking of every branch, every leaf skittering across the ground. Like there was nothing else in the world.

Sometimes I'm Becky Macomber

Sometimes, when I sleep over at Becky Macomber's house, I'm the first to rise. I look over at Becky, knowing she's still asleep, then I look up at the ceiling for the longest time, thinking about everything, because that's how I am. Afterward, I lift the sheets back, slide my legs out from underneath, and, for a second, it's like I'm getting ahead somehow, leaving Becky's bed with her sleep all trapped inside it and heading out, out past her parents' room, with its door half shut, and down the hardwood stairs where the Macombers' dog, Sherman, is lying against the bottom stair, locked in a dream, until I whisper his name and set him free.

We go into the kitchen, Sherman and me. There's this morning light that comes in through the kitchen curtains, all soft and churchy, and, even though I've seen it a dozen times before, it always surprises me, the way it doesn't mind me at all, with my socks all bunched down, and my hair unbrushed—it's like I've stumbled upon a wedding halfway through, and have been suddenly invited to be the bride.

The first thing I do is fill Sherman's bowl. I watch him for a while, then I open the refrigerator and just look and look. They've got everything in there, and I like looking at it, even though I know what I'm going to pick, but I just like looking, knowing I could pick anything, listening to Sherman going to town beside me. Then I reach for it: a glass jug of prune juice. It's heavy, and cold, but I can fit my hand around the neck. With the other, I twist the yellow cap.

Mr. Macomber has a thing about prune juice. They all tease him about it, even Becky, who has scribbled "YUCK" on the label with a thick black marker. Sometimes I take the bottle and hold it to my lips, not bothering to get a glass. The first taste is cold, wrong, but the juice warms in my mouth, disclosing its sweetness, pulpiness; it's really very tasty, although you'd never think so. Afterward, I put it back exactly where I found it, label out, cap tight.

And then there's something I almost always forget to do. I kneel down next to Sherman and put my hand to his head.

"Sherman the Wonder Dog," I whisper, "I wonder about you, Sher-man, I do," because that's something Becky says.

For a second his ears pulse in recognition, like he almost thinks it's her, then I feel an indifference in the smoothness of his fur and in the solemnity of his heavy tongue along the bowl, licking.

Sometimes, when I return upstairs, Becky is awake. "Where were you?" she'll ask.

"Bathroom," I'll say.

But she doesn't even say "Oh"—she just pulls the blankets around her, readjusting, finding sleep. Once she mumbled, "I dreamt you won a prize," but never brought it up again.

There's some famous saying about happy families being all alike, but I don't know what it is. Anyway, I know I can spot a happy family just by the layout of the living room, if that counts for anything. Here's what to notice: a coffee table with magazines on top (usually *Condé Nast* or *National Geographic*—unhappy families do not imagine travel); family photographs on the wall (not just posed shots, either, but regular ones, too, like someone licking pie off a plate, say, or standing in a parking lot waving a baseball cap); a blanket across the sofa (could be a quilt in an especially zealous case); some kind of plant life near the window (unhappy families need no reminder of death); and, most important, a TV that is hard to spot—usually in a cabinet, on a bookcase, or in another room altogether. If there's a piano in the room *and music on the stand*, you could be dealing with Laura Ingalls Wilder–type happy.

Of course, there's music on the Macombers' piano. It's the theme from *The Rose*—you know, the one about love being a river and everything, but when Becky plays it, she makes fun of it, rolling her eyes and singing dumb words, which kind of makes up for something.

Some say grub, it is a liv-er . . .

Sometimes Mrs. Macomber comes in from the kitchen, dish towel in hand, and joins in with goofy words of her own. That's another thing about happy families: they're always joining in, even if they're holding a damp towel.

Not Mr. Macomber, though. He's different. Quiet. He's got an office downstairs with one of those rolltop desks that no one has anymore, and that green-and-black saucer lamp you sometimes see in the movies when someone's paging through a medical record late at night, about to make a shocking discovery, while a guard watches from the doorway. *That* lamp. Sometimes Becky and I go down there to goof around, but we can never imagine what kind of game to make out of it all, all those props, so I usually just flick the lamp on and off for a while as Becky spins herself in her father's creaky leather chair.

When I'm with the Macombers, I get this feeling that I'm seeing something I shouldn't, like I'm about to figure something out, a way to be. So I listen. I observe. I watch them at dinner, talking about their day. They eat at the table (people really do). They light candles (not even a holiday). And they listen to one another. They joke. But it is in the silences between them that I feel it most, that I'm on the verge of something. I watch the way Mrs. Macomber passes the pepper grinder to Becky, the look with which Becky receives it, and hear the clink of Mr. Macomber's fork against his plate, and it's like they're all related in this crazy way, like the passing of the grinder and Becky's look and the clink are all one single gesture. I think about it for a while, until I feel ridiculous, me with my glass to my lips and all this weird feeling riding the back of my neck.

Once, they got into a conversation about almonds. Mr. Macomber asked Mrs. Macomber if she didn't used to put almonds in such and such dish, and Becky said she thought there used to be almonds, too, and then Mrs. Macomber said maybe she did used to put almonds in; she couldn't remember. Becky said, "I think I liked it better with almonds," and Mr. Macomber said he thought it was better without.

"Let's ask Jennifer," Mrs. Macomber said. "Which do you enjoy better? With or without?"

"I don't know," I said.

"I bet she enjoys it better with," Becky said.

Enjoy. The knowledge that that word could be used in conversation, that it was not just a billboard word, was like finding a seashell in a parking lot, all smooth and pink, whispering, listen, *listen.*

That night I listened to Becky falling asleep, her breathing. I closed my eyes, wanting to join her. I put my hands underneath the pillow, turned to one side, until I found a way, and followed.

I first met Becky at lunch. We'd been introduced once before, although it was obvious she didn't remember, but that was fine: she was only saving a seat for another friend and would be gone in a moment. She sat across from me, talking with friends at the far end of the table.

There are times so unremarkable in every way, so dull and ordinary, that, when looked back upon with the knowledge of their outcome, stand out like a dime run through the wash. I remember that Becky was leading the conversation for a while, being funny, loud, but then it passed to the other end of the table, where it stayed, with no immediate sign of return. We sat that way for a while, not saying anything, and it was like standing in line at the movies, or picking a fork from a drawer of silverware: nothing. The kind of nothing that makes up most of a day. A moment later the conversation came back to Becky, and she said something else, then stood from the table, giving up her seat.

Nothing.

But, still, in the time it took Becky to push in her chair I decided that we would become friends. It was like picking which shirt to wear, or whether to cut across a lawn instead of using the walkway—like that. And I remember feeling it the rest of the day, our friendship, as obvious and hidden as the socks beneath my jeans.

The television is front and center in our living room. There are no photographs on the wall. Our kitchen table is always covered with papers, letters, bills, receipts, notices; sometimes I put music on and sort through them, making little orderly piles out of it all. I like doing that. There's a fireplace in the living room that we never use anymore, and sometimes I take a pile of junk mail and put it inside, stacking it on the iron grating that's covered with soot and grime. I've been doing this for a while now, though no one seems to have noticed. I've even got a pizza box and three milk cartons in there, flattened, ready to burn.

Two birds live inside the chimney. At least it sounds like two.

I can hear them whenever I add to the pile, darting around above the flue. One makes a tiny, high-pitched *cheep*; the other, deeper, lower—I imagine this must be the mother. I've seen them from outside, too, landing on the chimney: heavy, black robins with twigs in their beaks. They look this way, then that, their bodies sleek, oily.

I always eat dinner in front of the television. I watch *Wheel of Fortune*. It's a terrible show, I know, but I like it anyway. I play a game with the theme music: if I sit down and take the first bite of my meal before the music ends that means good luck; if not—well, that's the thing: I never miss. I always feel a kind of triumph, taking that first bite with the music still playing and the sky getting dark. It's this crazy, strong feeling. I can't even describe it.

Once, I was shopping with Becky and Mrs. Macomber, Becky looking for school clothes. It had been a long evening, Becky couldn't decide on anything, and we had gotten into an argument about something or other, I don't remember what exactly. We walked apart from each other, taking opposite ways around jewelry kiosks and fountains, meeting in the center again, then nearly running so as to not be next to each other. Mrs. Macomber caught up to us.

"If you two are going to act like babies, you could at least crawl instead."

We studied our shoes, arms folded.

"Because that's what you two have been tonight. Infants." She walked ahead.

I remember thinking what a dumb thing it was for her to say, then feeling guilty for thinking that. I looked up at Becky, but she was already walking away. "Fine," I whispered, pretending she could hear. I was about to follow when I heard it.

The *Wheel of Fortune* theme music coming from across the way. A dim restaurant with a bar near the entrance, a television above, the bartender scooping ice into a plastic pitcher. I walked over and peered inside. There was hardly anyone inside except a few businessmen sitting at the bar, talking beneath the theme, sipping beers and saying things to the bartender who shook his head and offered pretend smiles. I watched them for awhile, not wanting to leave.

When the hostess leaned down to ask me what was wrong, was I lost? why was I crying? a sleepy voice arose from the bed of my lungs.

"I think I'm homesick," it said.

"One time I found my dad praying in the basement," Becky once told me. "It was a couple of years ago. I was real little then, but I remember walking by my parents' bedroom one morning and hearing them arguing about something. I couldn't hear much of it because the door was closed, but I put my head to the crack and listened. My mom was doing all the talking; my dad just made a few sounds here and there, enough to let me know that my mom wasn't sitting in an empty room talking to herself, but not much else.

"My parents almost never argued. It was strange, hearing it. At one point my mom raised her voice and said, 'Do you know what I need from you? I need you to tell me that I'm pretty sometimes. That's what I need.' Then I pulled away from the door because I heard someone rising from the bed and because I knew I shouldn't be listening and because my heart was going weird inside me.

"All day I kept thinking about it. *I need you to tell me that I'm pretty sometimes.* Whatever my mom did that day, whether she was reading a magazine or talking on the phone, I kept thinking that my dad was about to come in and say it. *You look pretty there on the sofa. You look pretty holding that pen.* But the day just went on as usual. We ate dinner like always. No one said anything.

"That night I crept down to the basement. The door was partly open and the lights were on. I knew all the places where the steps didn't creak. When I got halfway down I saw my dad sitting at his desk. He had his hands folded in front of him, eyes closed. I kept thinking that he was about to open them, but he didn't. He was praying. I'd never seen him do that before. I watched him for awhile. I watched him bring his hands to his face. I watched him move his lips without any words coming out of them. I watched him pray.

"When I went upstairs again, my mom was making my bed.

She spread the top sheet across the mattress and smoothed it with her hand, making it nice for me. Then she wrestled a new pillowcase over the pillow.

"I told her she looked pretty doing that."

Each day our bus passes a prison. From the highway it looks like any modern school building: red brick with long, narrow windows, basketball courts along one side, and a green lawn that stretches to a small forest behind it. The trees are like any other trees, the winds passing through like any other winds. In every way it is like any other building along the highway until you notice a wire fence that runs along the edge of the basketball court, around the parking lot, disappearing behind the other side of the building. On top, coils of barbed wire, silver and black, looking like waves crashing from the side. The fence is as high as a house.

Once we saw prisoners in the courtyard. It was a half day at school, and we had gotten out early. I sat next to Becky on the bus, looking out the window and thinking about nothing at all, if that's ever possible. When we passed the prison we saw them, just for a moment, playing basketball. They had blue uniforms on, not orange, not white, like you always see on television. There were prisoners playing on four different courts and prisoners standing off to the side, watching. When we passed I saw one man make a long three-point shot, the ball finding the bare hoop and passing through, noiselessly. It was a gorgeous day and the wind came in through half-open windows.

"Don't even think it," Becky said.

"Think what?"

"That it's nice. I know that's what you're thinking." She gave me a look. "It's a prison, Jenny."

But it was true, that *was* what I was thinking. Sort of. Not that it would be nice, necessarily, but that when the weather was like this, and you were outside with a basketball in your hands, ready to make a three-pointer, finding the shot and letting go, there had to be something in that. Not joy, not freedom, I guess, but something less than prison, for a moment. It's the way even the blackest, dismal asphalt can reveal washes of purple and veins of green in certain light. The way those colors are there, but aren't.

But Becky would never see it that way. She's not like that. If we're walking outside through the streets of her neighborhood, or crossing a lawn, and the day is warm, and there's a rightness in the sway of trees along property lines, with birds lighting on branches and taking flight again, and, as we pass into the high grass along the roadside, Becky finds an old crushed soda can underneath, she'll pick it up and carry it the rest of the way.

"Look at this can," she'll say.

I have not always told the truth. It was not Becky who saw her father praying in the basement. It was me. And it was not Becky who told her mother she looked pretty; it was not Becky who heard them argue.

That morning I woke early. I left Becky and closed the door behind me, slowly, my socked feet finding all the mute floorboards. I moved toward the Macombers' bedroom and heard them. I heard Mrs. Macomber. I heard her say, "Do you know what I need?" I heard all the rest.

I waited, wanting to hear Mr. Macomber say something. My heart was beating too big for my chest. I had this feeling. I felt that I was about to open the door, that it was about to happen, a certainty, that I would not be able to stop myself from doing so. I felt that I was about to enter the room. I put my hand to the knob, but didn't.

I found Sherman and headed into the kitchen. The morning light was there, but I couldn't feel anything about it. I kept thinking about the door. There was a scene in my head where I was telling Mrs. Macomber that she was pretty as Mr. Macomber said he agreed and Mrs. Macomber cried and Mr. Macomber cried and it was all because of me. I kept playing it over and over.

Then I opened the refrigerator and reached for the juice. I took the bottle in one hand and twisted the cap with the other. I raised the bottle to my lips and took in a long, cold drink. When I sensed a figure in the doorway, watching me, I turned.

Mr. Macomber was standing there in his bathrobe. He had a

look on his face that was not an angry look; his hair matted to one side, a cowlick in back. There was a softness to him in the morning light, in the hand that rested inside his bathrobe pocket, in the other that played with the end of the sash. He nodded at the nothing I did not say.

"It's so good," I said.

Mr. Macomber extended a hand and I gave him the bottle. When he took a sip it was like settling down to dinner in front of the television, the sky all dark, the theme just begun.

"No one believes," he said.

This
Day
in
History

June's grandmother took her to the mall, where the two of them stole a pair of red swimmer's goggles and ordered tuna clubs at the little restaurant next to J. C. Penney.

"Plus two Cokes," her grandmother said. "No ice." June pushed her menu toward the waitress and put her head to the table. She had always sort of liked it when teachers punished the class by turning out the lights and ordering them to put their heads down. It was okay in there, in that space between desk and arms.

"June, *hand* your menu back."

June sighed and lifted the menu from the table.

"You can tell everything you need to know about a person by the way they treat a waitress," her grandmother said. "How they were brought up, whether they had money, whether they didn't. Most people don't notice these kinds of things." She took a sip from her water glass. "Me, I notice everything."

June observed the waitress. She was about her mother's age, pretty, but with too many crows feet around her eyes. When she spoke, her voice was that of a teenager. "Oh sure," she said. "Today I had someone tell me he was going to write the manager a letter because we don't serve marmalade."

"A letter about marmalade," June's grandmother said. "I'd sure like to read that letter. Wouldn't you, June?"

June cupped her hands to her mouth. "The sun has landed," she said. "And our clothes are burning." She still had the goggles on.

Her grandmother turned to the waitress. "Lately I feel like we're all at the end of something," she said. "Do you ever feel that way?"

The waitress nodded. "They say it's because of the end of the century," she said. "But I've been feeling it for years."

The tuna club turned out to be soggy. June tried to squeeze out some of the excess mayonnaise, but it was no use. Her potato chips were wet on the bottom, too, but wet chips were wet chips, and June ate them anyway, imagining she was administering Holy Communion to herself, over and over again, until she ate the pickle, which didn't lend itself to anything you could imagine, unless you were disgusting, which she wasn't.

"Take those things off and try being a regular person," her grandmother said.

June ignored her, then realized she should have said "you first" when she had the chance. One day she was going to be one of those people who always knew the exact right thing to say at the exact right moment; it, along with her astonishing beauty, was going to sneak up on everyone when they least expected it, then— *pow*! But for now she watched her grandmother eat, and wondered if anyone had seen them stealing. There was a man reading the paper in the booth across from them, and June wondered if he was on to them, an idea she enjoyed. A headline on back of the man's paper proclaimed: "NEW ICEBERG IS BIGGER THAN DELAWARE."

Earlier, they'd parked their car along the avenue of cherry blossoms that lined the main mall drive. June's grandmother had just cut the engine when a wind sent a flurry of pink-white blossoms across the windshield, a few catching in the wiper blades and in the space between the hood and glass. June's grandmother let out a low, appreciative whistle.

"It's getting so the prettiest place is a parking lot," she said.

The weekend began with June's mother dropping her off in the driveway, the engine idling as June took her duffel bag from the backseat.

"She's watching from the kitchen window," her mother said. "Think I should wave?"

June told her she didn't care, wave all she wanted to.

"That would be something, wouldn't it? Me just waving and waving, saying howdy-do."

June closed the door.

"That was supposed to be a joke, honey."

"Ha-ha," June said.

A silence between them. The weight of the bag across June's shoulder. Her mother's foot upon the brake.

"I used to throw acorns over the garage," her mother said. "For hours. And I'd say to myself, 'If this acorn makes it all the way over, that means I'll go to heaven,' then I'd throw it and run around the other side to see if I'd be saved."

June knew she was supposed to ask "were you?" but she didn't feel like giving in. She watched her mother staring out at the garage and the trees beyond.

"Sometimes they were easy to find, just lying on top of the grass, you know, or under a bush. But every once in a while I'd throw one over and never find it. I mean, I looked everywhere but still nothing. Then one day I saw my father up on a ladder, cleaning out the gutters in back of the garage. He was pulling acorns out by the fistful and throwing them into a wheelbarrow, shaking his head, saying, 'Look at this! Can you believe all of this? Crazy, goddamned squirrels!'"

June walked around to the other side of the car and touched her mother's shoulder. "I'll call you on Sunday," she said.

"Sunday."

June gave her a kiss.

"Please don't think I'm a terrible person."

"Now why would I think that?" June said.

"Oh, I don't know. Lots of reasons, I guess."

When June reached the front porch, she saw her grandmother peering out from behind the curtain. She opened the door for June. "I could almost hear her nonsense from here," she said.

June spent her first afternoon reading catalogs in front of the television, while her grandmother vacuumed the spaces behind the sofa with a long attachment. It was her grandmother's way to invite you over for the weekend and then more or less ignore you, but June didn't mind. She liked reading through the catalogs and watching game shows on a day so sunny any other parent would have told her to go outside.

"Feet," her grandmother mouthed, and June raised hers. There was a pleasure in the passing of the vacuum beneath her feet, in the tension of her legs, and in the edge of tongue that peeked out from her grandmother's lips whenever she maneuvered the vacuum into a tricky spot. June watched her work, disappointed when her grandmother pulled the cord from the outlet and allowed the vacuum to swallow it again. The sound of the motor yawning into nothing suddenly depressed her.

"Don't you think it's too nice for me to be inside?" she said.

Her grandmother looked out the window, where summer was pressing in. "It could be," she said.

"I think maybe I'll go over to Ronnie's."

Ronnie lived in the house behind her grandmother's, a house as unremarkable as any other in the neighborhood except for the kidney-shaped pool in its backyard, a pool where June had often floated on a blue-and-white raft while Ronnie waded in, afraid to leave the concrete steps that initiated the shallow end. That Ronnie was in some way in love with her was evidenced by his attempts to leave this perch, one hand on the silver bar that sloped into the water, the other gripping the edge of the pool as his T-shirt billowed out around him, making him look much heavier than he already was. Ronnie's mother, Cathy, had watched the scene from a deck chair with a sad, rueful look. "You torture him, June," she said. "The poor boy."

And it was Ronnie's mother who now opened the door before June had a chance to knock. "She's back," she said.

"It's nice to see you again, Mrs. Mueller."

"Ronnie's up in his room pretending to be busy, so you won't think he's desperate." She motioned June inside. "He saw you coming across the lawn," she explained. "And 'Mrs. Mueller' lives in Detroit with seven cats that send their own Christmas card. Call me Cathy."

A moment later, Ronnie appeared at the top of the stairs, already wearing his bathing suit, flip-flops, and a pair of red swimmer's goggles that pinched his soggy head.

"We got him with box tops," Cathy whispered.

Outside, June found her familiar raft in the pool house, dusty but still limp with breath. Her breath? The idea fascinated her. She had a sudden notion to pop the air stem and suck it all back, but then Ronnie appeared in the doorway and said, "I found a quarter in the skimmer," and the notion passed.

They spent the next hour looking for coins in the shallow end. Ronnie, newly brave with his red goggles, dove underneath as June circled above on her raft, while Cathy read magazines beneath a patio umbrella that squeaked in the breeze. "They say if you haven't started saving food up already, it's probably too late," she said. Then, "Most cars won't start, either. Internal computers will think the engine hasn't been serviced since 1900." She laughed. "Can you believe that?"

"My grandmother has about a hundred jars of jelly in her basement."

"Great," Cathy said, "I'll stock mine with scones." She took a coin and tossed it into the water, the coin disappearing with a *plip*. Ronnie, tuned to that frequency, made an abrupt underwater turn and caught it as he surfaced.

"I'm rich!" he said.

Cathy found another coin and tossed it in. "People are already stockpiling champagne," she said. "Now *that's* hope."

June turned on her stomach and followed Ronnie's progress underneath the water. He reached for the coin, but it eluded him, pushed along by the force of his clumsy hand.

"When he's in those goggles, he thinks he's in another world," Cathy explained.

June watched as Ronnie's hand discovered the coin and trapped it, tight, secure. When he surfaced again, he held it up and said, "It's like I keep winning and winning."

The first store they tried was Sears. They wandered the boys section, then ended up in juniors, June's grandmother using the section displays as a guide. A canoe on the wall turned out to be a promotion for boys' jeans, and two girl mannequins frozen in a tennis match welcomed shoppers to athletic socks. "Half the point of being alive anymore is to drive everyone else crazy," June's grandmother said. "It really is."

They finally found the sports department, but there was only one kind of swimming goggles, sized "ADULT," with plain, clear lenses.

"I want colored ones," June said.

K-B was even worse, with boxes of toys strewn across the aisles and wild-eyed electronic animals that gyrated on plastic mounts and spoke in sentence fragments. "Time for a b-reak down!" a gorilla in sunglasses announced, then pawed a miniature keyboard.

"It's really coming," June's grandmother whispered. "It really is."

"Mrs. Mueller says that cars won't be able to start," June offered, but her grandmother didn't hear.

They found the swimming gear near the back of the store.

"Madness," June's grandmother said, reading the prices. "Just madness."

June crouched down and pulled a pair of goggles from the rack, then another, looking for a colored pair. It gave her a kind of thrill to hold so many in one hand, tossing aside the clear ones, a sense of anticipation and imminent success—she could see colored pairs from the side.

"I don't know which ones," she said, holding up two pairs of red, one labeled "ADULT" and the other "CHILD." "They kinda look the same." She tried holding the boxes to her eyes, but it was no use.

"They want to make fools of us," her grandmother said. She

took the "CHILD" package and put her thumb between the seam. "But we're no fools."

June watched, horrified, thrilled. It was like putting her head down in class. The moment the lights switched off, and her breath against her arms.

"Here," her grandmother said, stretching the goggles around June's head.

It hurts, June wanted to say, but couldn't.

"*Walk,*" her grandmother said, and June did. She walked. She walked out into the mall, out by the pay phones and people pushing babies in strollers, out by the skylights, out by the fountains applauding themselves over and over again, their bottoms jeweled with pennies.

"They want and they want," the voice said. "Look at them all."

She did. Red people, pushing, moving by.

"Makes you wonder what they want so want so bad, doesn't it?"

The hairs on June's forearms were straight as pins, prickly.

"More," the voice said. "They want *more.*"

Whenever she visited her grandmother, June slept in the room that had once been her mother's. The room had a twin bed flanked by pinewood nightstands, reading lamps on each, and a wide dresser with dolls on top, expressions frozen in eternal surprise. One of the first things June did whenever she unpacked was to turn each doll toward the wall, gently, smoothing dresses and straightening postures just in case the dolls were alive.

The second thing was to stare at herself in the mirror. Seriously *stare.* She didn't have a mirror in her bedroom at home—she had to limit her staring to the upstairs bathroom—but here, sitting on her mother's lumpy bed, June could go beyond, down into those deeper layers of staring she could only glimpse at home.

"I'll . . . die," she'd say along with Mirror June, wanting to feel something. "I'll die and Mom and Grandmom will cry. I'll die so young." Tears formed; she felt Mirror June's sympathy. If she concentrated, she could push Mirror June to cry.

"Everyone will feel sorry," she said, pressing her nose to Mirror June's, eyes wide, terrified. "*Everyone.*"

Her mother and grandmother had never gotten along. Before June's grandfather died, her grandmother would accompany him on holiday visits to her mother's house, but these were awkward events, her grandmother sitting in a straight-backed chair with a blanket across her knees, saying no to every seat, drink, cracker, chip, dip, pretzel, candy, and chocolate offered to her. When a present was handed to her, she'd remove the wrappings with a butter knife, then fold the paper back into reusable quarters.

After June's grandfather died, her grandmother stopped visiting altogether, and June's weekend visits began. June got her mother's duffel bag out of the attic and let it air on the clothesline. She picked out clothes she thought her grandmother might like to see her in: a green jumpsuit she'd never really liked, a sky-blue tank top, and a pair of overalls that still had a price tag on the inside. She liked the feeling it gave her, stepping out of her "real life" self and into this other June, the June who wore pastels, kid clothes.

Once, June found a flashlight tucked into the bag, a note attached. "Try shining this above the foot of the bed," the note read, in her mother's loopy script. "Love YOU! Mom." June lay with her feet on the pillow and shone the light onto the ceiling. At first, nothing: a white ceiling, whorls of paint, like a dull sky. Then, parts of the sky revealed themselves, glossy in the light, swirled into letters. H O W D Y ! they read, the W a sloppy butterfly, the Y a smile.

"Howdy," June said. She flicked the flashlight off and on.

There were some good spaces in her grandmother's house. You could go between the refrigerator and the range, where her grandmother kept extra grocery bags, if you were skinny enough. You could go behind the television, too, all dust and holes of light. But best of all was underneath the bathroom sink, where June could still manage to get her legs in—barely—knees drawn to her chest. She had an attachment to the items in there: a tube of bath oils, never opened, an oval of facial powder, and a coarse natural sponge that she used as a head pillow.

Once, June closed the doors just as her grandmother came in. She had been sniffing the oval powder puff when she heard her grandmother's slow, sighing footsteps, and she immediately pulled the door shut. A click of the light switch and the darkness was broken by a shaft of light between the doors, falling in a line across her tucked-up knees. For a moment she was afraid she was going to hear her grandmother use the toilet, but then she heard the faucet water singing through the piping and she relaxed a little. A moment later the water stopped, and June heard her grandmother sigh.

"Do you know why I don't climb underneath sinks?" she said.

June didn't respond.

"Because climbing underneath sinks is foolish, and I'm not a foolish person."

Sometimes June's mother fell asleep at the movies, even while the previews blazed. The sight of her leaning to one side made June feel she'd been forgotten.

"Mom," she'd whisper, "you're missing everything."

Saturday night they watched the late news together, June fighting to stay awake, her grandmother clipping coupons from a magazine. June watched her work the scissors, the television light making her look both dumpy and noble. She wanted to tell her grandmother to put the magazine away and go to bed, but the sound of the scissors gave her something to wrap her thoughts around, honey twirled onto a stick.

"I told Mom I'd call her tomorrow," she said.

Her grandmother nodded.

"To tell her what time."

"Somebody has to."

In the bedroom, June put the goggles on. They had been in her pocket since leaving the mall, clicking when she walked, poking her when she stretched out on the sofa. Now she greeted Mirror June—red Mirror June—with disapproval. She searched for words that would make them cry.

"Thief," she said, but there was nothing in it. She put her nose to the mirror. "End of the century," she whispered, then tried it again. She felt hairs on her forearms rise.

After a while, June heard her grandmother settling into bed. It was a cool summer night, and June lay awake and listened until she couldn't hear anything else except the whir of an electric fan in the next room. She flipped to one side and fell asleep to the noise. She dreamed of fast things moving by. She wished to touch them, but could not. Shadows and breezes revealed themselves to her, saying "See, *see?*"

A sound woke her. A scraping. It was still dark; light slanted in from her open door. June saw her grandmother standing before the dresser, in her lumpy robe, turning each doll back around as gently as she had faced them away. When she reached for the tallest ones, she held the folds of her sleeves back with her free hand.

"Grandmom?" June said.

Her grandmother stopped. "You don't love me," she said, flatly.

"Yes, I do," she whispered.

"No, you don't," her grandmother said, leaning a doll against the mirror. "But that's okay. That happens. You'll understand that one day." She sat down on the bed.

You shouldn't say things like that, June wanted to say.

After a while, her grandmother spoke. "Your mother used to love these dolls. Or at least I thought so at the time. We'd go to stores and pick out fabrics for dresses. We'd look through catalogs and pick out ones we wanted to get. Dumb things like that." A pause. "Then one time I found her crying in here. She had all the dolls in a cardboard box. 'Mom,' she said, 'I can't anymore. Please. Something's wrong with me. The new ones know I don't love them as much.' "

June watched her straighten a dress. "I bet Mom does," she whispered, "love you."

Her grandmother gave a little laugh. "Go back to sleep," she said.

But June couldn't. It would be daylight soon. A terrible fact.

June stood from her bed and walked to her grandmother's door. She could hear her sleeping, see the shape of her in her bed, ghostly in the early light. When she crossed the room, the floorboards neglected to creak. She put her hands to the edge of the bed. Her grandmother stirred.

"I can see in the dark," she mumbled.

"Me too," June said. She pushed herself up onto the bed and eased herself under the covers. There was a good space between the edge of her grandmother's pillow and her own, and she found it, relieved, tired.

When June woke, she found that her grandmother had made the bed around her, one pillow tucked in, the corners tight.

Sunday night her mother pulled into the driveway. June watched from the kitchen window, surprised when she stood from the car and closed the door.

"She's coming up the walk," June said.

Her grandmother gathered the newspaper from the table and carried it into the living room. She sat down and turned the television on, but June could tell she wasn't really watching.

June's mother knocked on the screen door, as June pushed it open and quickly handed her the duffel bag. "Hi," she said.

"In a rush?"

"No, I just—" and she stopped, because the look on her mother's face informed her that her grandmother was now in the kitchen, behind her. She felt the room shrink two sizes.

"Hi," June's mother said.

"Hello."

June stood between them, supporting the door, a door that would swing shut if she let it.

"I like what you've done to your hair," her mother said.

"Wig," her grandmother replied.

It was cool outside. Pink light caught in places across the walkway. June followed her mother to the car, knowing that her grandmother would be watching them from the window, like always. When they got to the driveway, June put her bag to the ground and picked a small black stone from the pavement. It was light and smooth, damp underneath. June raised her arm back, then lofted it high over the garage, sailing free of the roof and out of sight. She listened; it made no noise.